D1133122

JF
Quednau, Marion.
The gift of Odin

APR 0 4 2007

MID-CONTINENT PUBLIC LIBRARY
Dearborn Branch
206 Maple Leaf Ave
Dearborn, Mo. 64439

DE

WITHDRAWN
FROM THE RECORDS OF THE
MID-CONTINENT PUBLIC LIBRARY

The Gift of Odin

Marion Quednau

annick press
toronto + new york + vancouver

This story is dedicated to the real Odin and his favorite family with their ten good reasons.

Text © 2007 Marion Quednau

Illustrations © 2007 Sonja Mulabdic/Klik Creative

Annick Press Ltd.

All rights reserved. No part of this work covered by the copyrights hereon may be reproduced or used in any form or by any means—graphic, electronic, or mechanical—without prior written permission of the publisher.

We acknowledge the support of the Canada Council for the Arts, the Ontario Arts Council, the Government of Canada through the Book Publishing Industry Development Program (BPIDP) and the Ontario Book Publishing Tax Credit (OBPTC) for our publishing activities.

Edited by Barbara Pulling and Pam Robertson
Copy edited and proofread by Elizabeth McLean
Interior design by Vancouver Desktop Publishing Centre
Cover design by Sonja Mulabdic/Klik Creative
Cover and interior illustrations by Sonja Mulabdic/Klik Creative

Cataloging in Publication

Quednau, Marion, 1952–
    The gift of Odin / by Marion Quednau; illustration by Sonja Mulabdic.

ISBN-13: 978-1-55451-076-4 (bound)
ISBN-10. 1-55451-076-7 (bound)
ISBN-13: 978-1-55451-075-7 (pbk.)
ISBN-10: 1-55451-075-9 (pbk.)

    1. Potbellied pig—Juvenile fiction. 2. Potbellied pigs as pets—Juvenile fiction. I. Mulabdic, Sonja II. Title.

PS8583.U337G53 2007   jC813'.54   C2006-906155-6

Published in the U.S.A. by Annick Press (U.S.) Ltd.

Distributed in Canada by
Firefly Books Ltd.
66 Leek Crescent
Richmond Hill, ON
L4B 1H1

Distributed in the U.S.A. by
Firefly Books (U.S.) Inc.
P.O. Box 1338
Ellicott Station
Buffalo, NY 14205

Printed and bound in Canada

Visit our website at www.annickpress.com

D-CONTINENT PUBLIC LIBRARY

3 0000 12885657 6

MID-CONTINENT PUBLIC LIBRARY
Dearborn Branch
206 Maple Leaf Ave.
Dearborn, Mo. 64439

DE

One Good Reason

I know it's stupid to think that everything changed on a certain day at a certain time. It seemed harmless then, like seeing a fluffy white cloud and not knowing it was the first sign of a hurricane that would flatten houses— our house at least.

Okay, so Odin was rooting in my mother's garden. Eating her favorite flowers—her nasturtium. That's a Latin word pronounced "nass-ter-shee—YUM."

They were giant this year, in bright reds and yellows. And Odin clearly knew all about the "yum" part. I'd been putting petals into his food dish at suppertime, just to add a little flavor to his boring pellets.

Odin seemed to appreciate it—I could tell without him saying anything. Well, not in plain English. He grunts a lot, in different tones—he's the whole symphony, from flute to bassoon. Happy is usually low notes. But when he's worried—and Odin worries a lot:

about tall men, full moons, police sirens, the sound of the blender when I'm making fruit smoothies—he makes a high-pitched, shrieking noise in the roof of his mouth.

Odin is a Vietnamese pot-bellied pig. Except in Vietnam they don't grow to a hundred pounds plus—they get eaten when they get too big. My dad's told me that people there don't always have a local supermarket to pick up a few things for dinner. And sooner or later the family pig has to "bring home the bacon."

He was only teasing, or so I thought—until Odin waddled into the flowerbed. His super-saggy belly squished everything in his path that he hadn't already munched. So my mother threw a tantrum—that's what it looked like to me, anyway.

She shouted out into the backyard, "Give me ONE GOOD REASON to keep that pig!" Then she slammed the door, really hard, like I'm never supposed to do. Even by accident.

I didn't take it seriously at the time, but Odin started whistling through his teeth nervously. Sometimes he's smarter than I am.

Maybe my sister, Sonja, did it on purpose. Got me and Odin into trouble. She's the one who told me that certain blossoms—*especially nasturtium*—are served in salads in ritzy restaurants. And if I thought Odin was *so special* . . .

Sonja's five years older than I am. Seventeen, and

snooty. She mostly pretends I don't even exist. So it's hard to know when I'm going to bug her or not.

Like the other day, when my friend Pegga was over. We were putting nail polish on Odin's pointed little hooves—calling him Brad Pigg. We got the idea from one of Sonja's glamor magazines. Brad Pitt was on the cover looking oh so celebrity.

We found a greeny-gold color in Sonja's stash of make-up, and thought it suited Odin. Khaki-with-gold-flecks was his new hot-to-trot look. He didn't like the smell much, but he liked the company, the two of us huddled down with him, giggling our heads off.

When I heard Sonja come home—which is easy, because she's always complaining—I had to put the nail goo back in her room in a hurry. So I guess I left the top half-unscrewed. She bumped it on her dresser, and it spilled on her new neon-pink sweater. Now it has these green globs down the front.

Sonja was furious, of course. Right in front of Pegga she screamed at me: "Why are you even *alive*?"

"I think you should ask Mom and Dad," I said. Which didn't really help.

I don't think Sonja really wants me dead—but she isn't wishing a lot of good things for Odin. She says she's looking forward to Thanksgiving—the day Odin becomes a delicious roast ham, with crispy rind and pineapple on the platter. And then she smiles in a haunted way that's meant to scare me, says she's marking off the days on the calendar. It's as though she's developed a new kind of big sister mean streak.

Maybe my mom shouldn't have given her that fancy-schmancy name. She must have seen it in one of her romance novels or something. *Saaaanja, daaarling Saaanja.* No wonder she's always painting her toenails some new shade called Ochre or Black Cherry, and watching Entertainment TV, as though she's somehow related to the stars.

I have a ham-and-cheese sort of name. Tammy. It sounds down to earth, like someone who'd be a good friend. Even to a pig named Odin.

Lately Odin's been in pig heaven, eating the mushy apples falling to the ground under our old apple tree. Not to mention vegetable peelings, stale bread, and anything in the fridge that's gone yucky, even old soup. To hear him slurping up chicken noodle leftovers is something else. He likes it lukewarm, the way he likes his water too. He actually tips his rubber bowl to get the very last drop.

He's a natural composter. Which is one good reason to keep Odin. I should let my mother know. I should just give her a Tammy Speech and say: Forget the slop bucket of rotting food under the sink and taking it out to the compost bin in the backyard. The raccoons always get into the plastic container anyway, no matter what we do. Odin's far more efficient. That's what I should say.

Except then she might remember how he bumped open the fridge with his snout and got into the veggie drawers, making his own personal coleslaw. My mom insists Odin's been the cause of a lot of "kerfuffle" around here. She uses all these old British expressions. She says Odin's "peckish" when he's hungry, and complains that the weather's getting a "tad" cold to keep a pig in the backyard.

"Notice we don't have a barn," she said to me the other day, as though it's my fault they don't allow farms with neat stuff like chickens and horses and pigs in the city.

Odin's favorite spot to hang out is by the back steps—he's made a trough there that gets sloppy when it rains. When it's sunny, he's flat out, snoring. Well, not exactly flat, more like a big, gray balloon. He actually looks insulted if we interrupt him from a nap, ask him nicely to shove over.

My mom keeps swearing someone's going to forget he's there and trip over him, go head over heels. I don't see how anyone could miss seeing Odin.

Or hearing him. Odin knows exactly what he likes and doesn't like—he's got opinions. And he's a real comedian. Like the time he got tangled up in the living room drapes. He looked like some sort of a magic show gone wrong; instead of white doves or a rabbit, out came a big, fat pig with a surprised look on his face. We all keeled over laughing.

But that was then and this is now. When no one at my house is exactly in a mood of hardy-har-har.

Lately my dad's keeping a "stiff upper lip," according to my mother. That means he's trying to cope.

My dad's been bored and grumpy because he wants to get back to work. He mostly sits in the living room with his bad leg up on the sofa and the newspaper up around his face. The doctor says it'll be weeks before he's off crutches, then walking with a cane.

He's the safety supervisor down at the sawmill. The carriage—this thing that guides huge tree trunks into the blades—got stuck, and when my dad tried to fix it, logs spilled everywhere. That's how my dad wrecked his leg and his hip.

It's weird, because the day before my dad's accident, everything seemed perfect. It was still summer holidays, but for some reason I got up early to walk down to the train station with him. I know commuters do it every day, and grumble about it. But to me it seemed exciting. The two of us standing on the platform, the train screeching into the station with that hot rush of air.

Now I feel like it's the last time I saw the father who used to make jokes all the time. He was constantly playing pranks—just like a big kid. As if a part of him forgot to grow up. Once we had a volleyball tournament that lasted weeks—inside the house! We'd surprise each other with spiking and shooting, and left round smudges all over the walls. I mean, if that isn't the ideal kind of dad, I don't know what is.

My dad never used to get frazzled about things going a little wrong. But lately he's been moody—I guess 'cause he's not going to work. And my mom's had to go back to nursing full-time to take the pressure off my dad. She's always zooming around like she's in some sort of emergency, even at home. Sometimes she forgets to take her uniform off, as if the people in her family have become her worst patients. Maybe that's why she was shouting at Odin.

And then there's Sonja—"languishing," as my mother describes it. I have no idea what that means, except that my sister's basically stopped eating and has a squinty, faraway look in her eye, as though she's staring directly into the sun.

Sonja, sighing girl, out-of-love girl, putting on airs of great tragedy.

She got Odin in the summer as a birthday present from her then-boyfriend, Sam. It's too early to be thinking about getting serious, my mother told her, when she heard Sonja had received a *big, fat gift* from Sam. That's how I put it, just to be funny.

I suppose my mother thought it was a string of pearls or a trip to Vegas or something. She acted as though Sonja was getting married, and went off on a rant about girls having it better these days, how there was no reason to settle down with the first boy you meet. How Sonja should go to college first.

I always thought Sam was pretty neat, and this Odin thing cinched it for me. Instead of a stupid ring, this guy gives her a real, live pig. One he really *liked*—as if he wanted to share the way he felt about the world with Sonja.

He'd rescued Odin from a pet shop for exotics, animals from foreign countries and other climates, cockatiels and iguanas, huge pythons, you name it, all in cramped cages. And there was Odin, looking miserable as could be, right next to a hissing serval cat from Africa.

Sam said Odin was a lucky kind of gift, changing bad karma to good.

"What's karma?" I asked.

"Well, karma is like your fate—and you affect it by what choices you make. So, it's also a mood or atmosphere, something you carry with you. Like the way you feel good when you've done something right, and not so good if you've screwed up. And how one action leads to others—it may seem like luck, but it's really the fact that you did the right—or wrong thing—in the first place, " Sam said.

It sounded a little confusing, but I think I get it. Sam meant that how you act affects everything around you. And anything that Sam says, well, you have to believe him. It's because of his eyes, so dark brown they almost seem sad. That's how you see the serious side of him. If you just notice his wild hair, sticking out all over like a hedgehog—black, with these crazy bleached blond streaks—well, you might not know right away who Sam really is.

But Sonja, she wasn't impressed. Instead of looking deep into Sam's eyes and giving him one of her slithery hugs—she burst into tears. Refused to even touch Odin.

Okay, so Odin's not exactly as cuddly as a kitten. His skin's like flabby concrete, with bristly hairs sticking out. And he has a jowly face—he can make his eyes almost disappear when he wrinkles his nose up. He wiggles his snout around like a vacuum hose when he snuffles in the dirt for goodies like earthworms or shiny black beetles. He even eats slugs—it's positively gross. Especially when he's frothing and smacking his lips a little.

Maybe that's what Miss High-and-Mighty was thinking when she turned her own snobby nose up at Odin—and broke up with Sam too. Just like that.

It's crazy, because they were almost obsessed with each other. I never noticed doorways before those two starting hanging out in each and every one of them, kissing hello or goodbye or just because.

Now summer's over and school's started again and my mother's tired and my father's Mr. Grumpy and my sister's flipping out and no one wants to keep Odin. No one except me.

2

Pig Opera

I'm not sure that even Pegga has a lot of enthusiasm for Odin. I mean, she knows I think he's the best. But she doesn't really get it, either.

Maybe she thinks Odin's a stage I'm going through, like when she wanted to become an opera star. Last year she took singing lessons, and got all strange on me. She'd sing everything back to me, at the top of her lungs. Stupid things, like "I told you sooooooo!" Or "Are you hungryyyyyyyy?" I finally said to her, I thought opera singers were all sort of . . . *fat.* Did she want to look like that?

I think she was mad at me for a while. I mean, it would be a real stretch to imagine a chubby Pegga. She's actually skinny—a size nothing—and can do cartwheels without blinking an eye. About as opposite to me as you can get. I'm "bigger-boned," as my mom calls it, always bumping into things or spilling things, as if I don't quite know where my body begins or ends.

But right now the two of us are both fatties—well, the *three* of us.

Pegga and I are lying down on either side of Odin in the backyard. We're trying to keep him busy. He's lately gotten a taste for sunflowers too. Good thing it's the end of the gardening season; soon the backyard will be nothing but weeds and bare patches.

We've each got two pillows duct-taped round our stomachs so that we're super-plump. To give ourselves fatter heads, we've squished rolled-up gym socks into our hoodies, with the draw-strings pulled tight round our faces, scrunching up our eyes.

I look at our shadows on the grass. Not bad. We look like three not-so-little piggies by our hunched outlines. And this is definitely to Odin's liking—he's humming a little, making his gurgly, happy noise.

But Pegga's squirming, says the cushions are making her too hot.

"Think how Odin feels," I say. "He can't take his flab off later."

I have a feeling Pegga's not that keen on making herself into a pretend pig. She keeps thinking she feels bugs in her hair, even though her hood's so tight she can hardly breathe. I have to admit she has the most beautiful hair, so straight and thick and shiny she could do shampoo ads on TV. Not like mine, all frizzed out, except when I'm playing pig and have it pressed down.

"I can't see anywhere but straight ahead, how 'bout you?" Pegga says. "It's weird. Like a thin slice of the view, not the whole thing."

"Everything's kind of blurry," I say. My squeezed-up eyes make the whole backyard look somehow underwater.

"Why are we doing this again?" Pegga asks.

"We're trying to see things from Odin's point of view," I remind her.

Pigs are near-sighted and built low to the ground, so they're top-heavy on short legs. It's good for snuffling around for treats, but you have the pig worry of being too fat and comfy to get out of the way of anyone who doesn't like you. Which could be right now.

We see feet approaching—fast—heading straight for us. I can see Pegga's shoulders shaking, as though she's got hiccups or the giggles. But we lie low, pretend to be a HUMAN-PIG-HUMAN speed bump.

I can tell who it is by the shoes: white, thick-soled nursey ones.

Although my mother's short, from where we are—hunkered down with Odin—she towers over us. Odin half sits, alarmed. He doesn't like anyone hovering above him, casting any kind of a shadow. It's an old instinct, I guess, from being thought of as lunch in the

14

wild. Things like ancient tigers and hyenas, and people with spears, chasing after you.

"Tammy, *what on earth* are you doing?"

The Voice seems to be coming from some distant place—it's hard to hear through all the padding over our ears. Odin's hearing is just fine, though, and he starts to mutter nervously.

Pegga pulls the socks out of her hood. "Hey, Mrs. Gifford, how's it going? Isn't it beautiful weather? I mean, for autumn?"

Pegga has what my mother calls "good company manners." She knows just what to say in a pinch. Maybe it runs in her family—they're Korean and always seem to be super polite to each other.

"Yes, it is a nice day, Pegga," my mother says.

I'm trying to read whether her smile is a Number 1 or a Number 2.

My mother's Number 1 smile: mouth tipped up at both ends like a canoe, dimples in her cheeks. Meaning, you're a hopeless kid for forgetting to do the dishes or start supper. But I love you anyway. Anything I say right now is just teasing.

My mother's Number 2 smile: a fake version of the first. Mouth pressed together, trying to lift up at the edges. Too tight to make it. Meaning you're pressing on some nerve that keeps her from using her real smiley face, and she doesn't actually feel good at all. It's a warning.

Pegga's standing now. With the cushions taped to her front, she looks all blown up, like a pregnant skinny kid. My mother looks shocked for a minute.

Then Pegga unzips her sweater and starts ripping the duct tape off the cushions. I can't believe she'd do this right in front of my mother. I'm rolling my eyes, trying to stop her.

"I have to go—" Pegga says. "You know, help my mom with the yoga class down at the rec center." She's rip-ripping, tearing some of the fuzz off the fabric. Then she plops the cushions onto the ground.

"Are those the *good* cushions—from the living room?" my mother asks.

There's suddenly a whole new category of not-quite smiling on her face. A Number 300: face freeze-up. Her eyes have a kind of eerie, tinfoil shine to them.

"Tammy, what were you *thinking*?"

"We were trying to imagine what it's like to be Odin," I say. I'm round and plump, sitting up beside him. I'm also starting to sweat like crazy.

My mother is staring at me with disbelief. Or maybe it's pity, as if she's feeling sorry for me—or for Odin. Or maybe both of us.

Pegga's walking backward out of the yard, keeping her eyes on me the whole time. Her expression seems to be saying, *Tammy, keep your mouth shut, be careful.* But she's not sticking around to see what happens next.

My mother's making that weightlifter sound, the same grunt she makes when picking up dishes or dirty laundry off the floor in my bedroom. She's making a big deal out of shaking the cushions, slapping them to loosen the small clods of dirt and dead leaves.

"Has it ever occurrrr—ed to you—" she asks, the "urr" part all stretched out, like a growl, "that Odin might not be happy here?"

Not happy? What is she talking about?

Scenes flash into my head of the summer just past . . . Sam balancing a plum on Odin's nose and Odin making goofy faces; Odin scratching himself on the edge of the outdoor barbecue, his tummy making that velcro sound on the bricks; Odin stretched out on the oval rug in the kitchen as though he owns the place. In every single scene Odin's having the best time, just being the center of attention. And everyone is laughing along with him.

Of course, that was when everyone at our house *was* still laughing. At all.

A new wave of heat is making the back of my neck sticky. I feel all prickly, as though I've fallen into a patch of stinging nettles.

"That's so unfair—" I gasp. "He's the happiest pot-belly ever!"

"How do you *know* that, Tammy? How can you be so sure?"

Odin raises his lips and bares his teeth a little. I can tell he wants to say something. He looks so helpless, his front legs spread wide like he's doing the pig splits.

I grab a strip of the ripped-off duct tape Pegga left behind, and plaster it over my mouth. Then I squeeze my eyes half-shut and produce a blood-curdling scream from behind the tape. So loud my head feels like it's going to explode.

"Tammy, try to act your age—" my mother says. Then she strides toward the back gate, holding her precious sofa cushions up to her chest, lifts the latch and closes it so hard behind her, the gate vibrates with a rat-tattle-tat-tat.

My age is almost thirteen years old. And I have to say that in all that time—twelve years and nine months—I've never seen my mother walk into the back alley in a huff, and then disappear. This is definitely a first.

I run into the house, push my pudgy shape past my dad. He's limped over to the screen door to see what all the fuss is about. And Sonja's standing right behind him, smirking. I moan at her in a muffled voice and lock myself in the bathroom.

I look in the mirror and can see I'm crying, although I can't quite feel it. The duct tape was a mistake—it feels as though I have sunburned lips when I rip it off. There's a big red area around my mouth. Great. I look like a clown. Especially with the lumpy padding still fastened around my middle. I unzip my hoodie and rip the tape off, leaving sticky streaks on the cushions. Good, I think.

Even without the pillows, I don't like the picture.

Now that my hood's off I watch my hair spring up all over my head. I look like I've been electrocuted or something. That's how I feel too—zapped.

I tilt my head, turn a little and try to look over my shoulder at the image. I stand on the edge of the bathtub and look again. Mirrors are a pain—you can never see your whole body. It's either tops or bottoms, one side or the other, always at some crazy angle. Right now my sports bra's bunching up behind as though I'm a hunchback, and my hips look all squished together with my waist, in sort of smudgy layers. If I look like this to anyone else, I must seem hopeless. As if I can't even dress myself and keep the whole picture together. Not without duct tape, anyway.

My murky gray-green eyes aren't anything special, either, although they sometimes change color if I'm excited or upset. Like right now. Then they seem much brighter, almost Jell-O green. That's what Sonja called them once. Whatever.

And then there's the issue of freckles. Some days I

don't even see them, and sometimes they seem to stare out from my face like an ugly brown rash.

"Freckles, shmeckles," I say, looking out the bathroom window.

I can see Odin's head among my mother's sunflowers. He's going to munch the whole lot down. That's his way of having the last word, I guess.

I can also see my mother's head, nodding at someone. She's two yards down, talking to Mrs. Trimble. Good, I think. She'll be awhile.

Mrs. Trimble and my mom have a lot in common. They both spent part of their childhood in England, and remember trips to the seaside and when you bought fish and chips wrapped in newspaper, that sort of thing.

So now the two chit-chatting mothers can have a good talk about me. How I prefer the company of pigs to some people. How I can't even keep Odin out of trouble. How I can't be sure Odin is even the slightest bit happy.

3

Project Happiness

I know that kids like to make fun of teachers, but I happen to like Miss Diana Pickles. I get the feeling she wants us all to do well. Her motto is: "Try—and the sky's the limit." She says this in a sing-song voice that makes it rhyme a little. It gives me faint hope that I might actually enjoy English class this year.

Some kids call her Miss Picky, and others, The Dill. Sometimes Pegga and I just call her Diana, to save her the embarrassment of her last name. We figure she's suffered some kind of a tragedy, and that's why she dresses the way she does—in velvet jackets or frilly blouses, with long skinny skirts and lace-up granny boots. And every one of her outfits, day after day, is purple. Not the pastel kind, but a deep plummy color—so her name could actually be Miss Diana Purple. Even her reddish hair, pinned up in a bun like a ballerina, has a purplish tint, and her glasses have pointed tips with jewels on them—"amethysts," Pegga says. But all I know is that they're purple.

We heard Pegga's mom talking about Miss Pickles to a friend. How Diana thinks of her students like her own children, and with her having no chance for a family . . . They changed the subject when they knew we were eavesdropping. But that's how Pegga and I got the idea that some guy with an Elvis hairdo had left her long ago, maybe back in high school, and she'd never gotten over it.

I'm beginning to know all about tragedy. For my mother to even pretend she wants me to get rid of Odin *for his own good*—

Pegga makes signals from across the aisle—she wants to pass me a note. When Miss Pickles turns to write something on the board, I hold my palm open.

Pegga has scrawled, "*What hapenned yesturday?*"

She's not the world's best speller, but sometimes she can almost read my mind. I don't want to share my mom's latest theory about Odin, so I just shrug. Then etch a pig face on the paper, with a glum look, and then another pig, with a happy face.

Miss Pickles is explaining our first major assignment for the year. We each have to give an oral presentation.

Everyone moans.

"It's not that hard," she assures us. "You talk all day long, don't you? In the halls, at lunch, after school? Hmm?"

More moaning.

Miss Pickles continues in the same cheerful voice, as if she's announcing a holiday or a field trip. "You can use everyday language, as though you're explaining something to friends. But you have to research your subject and gather up your thoughts," she warns us. "Or else three to four minutes will seem an awfully long time."

Miss Pickles points to the board. "Does everyone understand what this means?"

She's written: *How we can be good stewards for the earth.*

Walter Cluster blurts out—"Oh, you mean taking care of it properly. Not throwing our garbage out the car windows, not even driving a car if we can walk or bicycle . . . that kind of thing."

Diana's actually getting dimples, she's so pleased with Walter's answer.

"Yes, thank you, Walter Cluster."

Everyone speaks to Walter by using his last name too. That's just the way you deal with him. He doesn't seem to mind. In fact, he doesn't seem to mind getting the best marks in the class or falling asleep in the middle of gym when we're supposed to be vaulting or running laps. Or wearing long-sleeved, pinstriped shirts, even in warm weather.

Miss Pickles starts click-clicking on the blackboard again with her chalk.

I shove my hand into the aisle, open my fingers. Bad timing. Pegga's hand isn't there to receive the note, and the white scrap of paper flutters to the floor one desk back, at Walter Cluster's feet. I hear him snort. For Walter, that can be a happy sound, like it is for Odin.

Walter slides the note just out of my reach with the toe of his running shoe.

"I'd like you all to choose something intriguing about the world you live in. Not anything you know a great deal about, but some new subject. You have to explore a little," Diana says brightly.

A whole class of would-be explorers looks blank.

"How do we know what we don't know, until we know it?" Walter asks. Everyone laughs. Walter's famous for his lame questions.

"Let's take trees as an example," Diana says. "And the way they clean the air. Every time we cut down too many, and put too many shopping malls in their place, we lose twofold . . . If you don't know how this works, maybe one of you could find out."

Of course, right away, everyone wants to do the same topic—trees galore.

Miss Pickles is printing the word "TREES" on the board, the big bun on the back of her head bobbing a little. I'm half-falling out of my seat, swatting at Walter's leg.

"Who wants to go first?" Miss Pickles asks, pivoting on her heels, and beaming out at the class, as though we're all her best students.

I *know* she catches a glimpse of me finally snatching the note back. So I shoot my hand up in the air like a keener. Someone like Missy Miles. Her hand's always waving about like some reaction she can't help.

"Tammy, you? That's wonderful—Now does everyone understand what we're doing?"

I myself haven't the faintest idea what we're doing, or why I just volunteered.

I'm suddenly twitchy, wondering whether my dad remembered to feed Odin his lunch. Or whether Odin's got himself into some new kind of trouble, if he seems neglected, underfed. Or overfed. Too round and roly-poly. I get this horrible ice-cubey feeling in the pit of my stomach and wonder whether Odin's life at that moment is absolutely perfect. Or perfect enough to keep my mother happy.

I try to concentrate.

"Now, our little chats—starting with Tammy's—will begin right after Thanksgiving. Mark it on your calendars, so you don't forget!"

Everyone groans again. Everyone except Walter Cluster.

"Good thing I love speeches," he says. He's grinning his head off. He's such a geek.

"W.C. is a real scream," I write, making sure Pegga

has the note firmly this time, like a paper baton in a relay.

"Not," she scribbles, and shows it to me across the aisle.

Underneath my pig faces she's drawn a long, swoopy dress on the glum one, and a mini-skirt and some clunker high-heel shoes under the happy-faced one. And she's written *Miss Diana Piggles* . . .

I scrunch up my face at Pegga—I don't think we should be making fun of Miss Pickles. Walter Cluster yes, Diana no.

I can see Walter reach his long, thin arm over Pegga's shoulder to grab the note. Pegga gasps loudly. Miss Pickles turns, holding her chalk in midair. She smiles at a point directly behind Pegga's head.

Everyone in the room is snickering, but Walter is hunched over his desk, scribbling, totally oblivious. Miss Pickles walks so quietly down the aisle, on her tippy toes, she might *really* have been a ballerina at one time.

"Thank you, Walter Cluster."

Walter places the scrap of paper slowly into her open palm.

Miss Pickle's eyes move slowly over the note. Pegga is sliding down into her seat, blushing so hard she looks like she's having heat stroke.

We expect Miss Pickles to yell at us, say something about us acting childish, or her feeling shocked, something. Instead, she smiles at us in turn, at Pegga, at Walter, and then at me, as if we're points on a hopeless triangle. Then she recites in a calm, clear voice:

"'The time has come,' the Walrus said,

'To talk of many things:

Of shoes—and ships—and sealing wax—

Of cabbages—and kings—

And why the sea is boiling hot—

And whether pigs have wings.'"

The whole class looks stunned. As in, has Miss Pickles gone bonkers?

"Walter Cluster—" she says finally, "do you happen to know who said that?"

Walter grimaces, shakes his head. "Can't say that I do," he says. Even brainy Walter Cluster doesn't know something for once.

"Lewis Carroll—at least that was his pen name. He was a mathematician, who became famous for a story he wrote for his seven-year-old niece, *Alice in Wonderland.*"

"Ohhhhhhh," Walter says. "I thought it sounded familiar."

"But the Walrus appears in *Through the Looking Glass,* another of Carroll's works. It's really quite fun to read," Miss Pickles explains.

She keeps her tone sweet as maple syrup when she adds, "You three will drop by after school, won't you? Don't disappoint me—I'll be expecting you."

She walks to the front of the classroom so quietly the sound of a pen dropping makes us all startle in our seats. Walter Cluster's, of course.

We stand outside the closed door to room 202 and listen. Not a sound. No one wants to knock to find out if she's actually there.

"Maybe she's gone home to rake leaves," Walter says.

"Shut up, Walter Cluster," I hiss at him in a loud whisper. "As if you haven't done enough already . . ."

"She must be *mortified*," Pegga says, clutching at her chest like she's having a seizure. "I got that expression from reading a creepy mystery. It means shocked, outraged, about to faint. Isn't it great?"

I have to wonder about Pegga sometimes.

We don't even hear footsteps—but suddenly the door opens. Pegga gasps. She's had a real gasping day.

"Come on in, I was just finishing some marking," Diana says, with this amazingly warm smile, as though she's enjoying the pleasure of our company at three in the afternoon.

"I want to explain—" I blurt out, "about Odin."

"What's an Odin?" Walter asks.

"Odin's a pig—I have a pig."

"You have a pig?" Diana asks, with genuine interest.

"Yes, I do," I say. "I have a Vietnamese pot-bellied pig."

It feels good to be saying it out loud, like a vow or something. Even if it's only in front of Walter Cluster—and Pegga, who already knows—and Miss Diana Pickles, who now probably hates me for making fun of her. Although I didn't.

I give Pegga an accusing look, so that she'll admit she was the one to draw the Miss Piggles pics. But all Pegga does is open and close her mouth a few times, like a goldfish. I don't want to tell on her, so I just keep talking about Odin.

"Odin came from a shop for exotic pets—they're often kidnapped, right out of the jungle or somewhere, and sent to places in the world where they don't belong, so someone can have a python in his living room just to be cool. Or maybe a beautiful cockatiel who starts losing all his feathers, he's so unhappy."

"Is that why you have a pig, just to be cool?" Walter asks.

Pegga laughs nervously. I give her another dirty look.

"Why *do* you have a pig?" Diana asks. She raises one of her red, sketched-in eyebrows.

I hesitate. This is really my mother's question, coming out of Diana Pickles' mouth.

"Well, otherwise he might have died from loneliness, I guess, or a bad diet that didn't suit him. Or from nervous habits animals get when they're too cooped up, like howling or pacing in circles—"And then I say, more firmly, "Nobody else knows how to care for him the right way."

Behind her pointy glasses, Miss Pickles' eyes are blue, pale blue like a baby's. It's as though she can see straight through you.

"It sounds as if you care a great deal for Odin," Miss Pickles says.

To me, in that moment, she's more a Diana, a real friend, than any stuffy sort of a Miss Pickles.

She clicks her tongue on the roof of her mouth as though she's about to say something more, and then changes the subject. "Consider yourselves lucky—you three are getting a head start on those speeches," she says cheerfully. "You can go to the back of the room and rummage through the books I've collected from the library—see if any of the topics tickle your fancies . . . ."

Pegga and Walter go whispering to the back of the room, opening and closing books, pages flapping. I just stand there like an idiot and press my eyes shut. For some reason I feel like I'm about to cry and I don't even know why.

"And Tammy—you already have an idea for a topic, right? That's why you offered to go first?"

"Right," I mumble.

I plunk myself down at a desk, my eyes blurring.

I wish it was summertime again, when my mother wasn't always rushing around in some state of emergency, working crazy shifts. And my dad wasn't in gloom-city. And my sister was half-decent to me. *Half*-decent. When almost anyone could drop in for dinner. Including Sam, who'd almost always bring Odin along on his leash. At least until the day *Saaaaanja* had her hissy fit and ran into the house crying.

Sam looked hurt, big-time, so I stepped in, said I'd *gladly* take Odin.

"Great," Sam said, although he looked like he wanted to run and hide under a rock. "That's great, Tammy."

And he handed me the leash to Odin's harness, and that was that. It was like musical chairs, and the tinkly music stopped, and everyone but Sam got a seat at our house.

It was all a huge mess, with my mom sort of relieved that Odin wasn't a glitzy ring, but hoping, too, that Sam and Sonja would make up. And all my dad said about a pig suddenly living with us was that Sam had to "save face." Which means that Sam's pride had been squashed.

Before that prickly moment, summer had been a breeze. Easy and fun. Often we'd eat in the backyard, at the picnic table, Sam sitting too close to Sonja, so their arms were bumping all the time. And Pegga was always welcome too.

"Everyone slide over," my dad would say. "That girl with the huge appetite's here." Meaning tiny little Pegga.

I remember the day my dad was grilling pork chops on the barbecue, and Odin wanted to make sure we all knew he disapproved. He wrinkled up his nose until it practically did a back flip.

"It's as though he's inviting US into HIS backyard, not the other way around," my mother said—my *old* mother, the one who used to put up with Odin's moods. She actually used to spray him with the hose when the weather was hot and dry, and make a puddle for him. She'd pretend not to mind him mooching for food or asking to have his tummy rubbed while she was running back and forth to the house.

Nowadays Odin's getting a lucky break if he makes it as far as my room, which my mother calls a pigsty, even though it's not any messier than usual. She's known all along that I sneak Odin in there sometimes, so he can hunker down in my dirty laundry, or snuffle around for cast-off chip bags or browned apple cores. Once my mother didn't mind—and now she does.

Everything's changed and I can't figure out how to fix it.

I realize then that Pegga and Walter are packing up their books and heading for the door. Pegga gives me a "Hurry up!" look. She doesn't notice that my eyes are a bit swimmy.

"We have to wrap things up now, Tammy," Diana says. "I'm late for a meeting." She says it so patiently I almost forget I had to stay after school in the first place.

Pegga and Walter have already disappeared—I can hear them laughing their way down the hall. And I suddenly have this crazy idea.

"I might have to find Odin a new home," I blurt out. "So I have to find out more about Vietnamese pot-bellies, to be really sure what makes Odin happy. Can that be my project? Remember—how you said we had to explore?"

"Does your idea relate to the environment?" Diana asks gently. I think she can feel I'm on the verge of losing it. She has to say yes, or I'll burst into tears.

"Well, Odin had a whole season of plums, and apples, and he wallows in his trough by the back door, makes his own sort of pond to cool off. Pigs can overheat easily," I say. I'm talking so fast my words are all blurring together. "And he's the world's best composter, eats anything we can't use."

"Well, it sounds as if you have a topic—" Diana says slowly, as if she's thinking about it. "I think there might be some books about—your friend—at the library downtown. You could take a look."

"Thanks," I say.

And suddenly I'm not feeling so desperate. Even the thought of Pegga and Walter Cluster getting us in trouble doesn't seem so bad anymore. Odin is going to get me a good mark in English, maybe an A for once. Second good reason to keep Odin. Odin as big, fat oral presentation.

I can actually picture myself at the front of the class—using maps and chalk and a pointer, like Diana does, clicking it against the board for effect.

"I have to get going," Miss Pickles says, snapping her briefcase shut.

"So do I," I say. "I have to walk and feed Odin—he'll be waiting."

I can almost hear him already. He always gives a little high-pitched shriek when he sees me after school. It's a bit like the screeching of the sea gulls that fly along with the ferry when we go to see my grandma. It's a mooching-for-french-fries and happy-to-see-you sound all rolled up into one. Odin's voice swoops up and down a little like a gull's too.

My mother's *not* right—about him being unhappy. I'm Odin's friend, after all. The only one he has left, it seems. I'll read up all about his likes and dislikes, and then explain to the class—to the whole world—what makes him tick. Odin's real purpose in life, why he exists at all. What makes Odin happy.

My mother can't get rid of my best ever school project. That wouldn't make sense. Too bad it isn't further away. I suddenly wish I hadn't offered to go first.

4

Fortune Cookie

Pegga and I are making a big deal of swaying back and forth on the downtown bus every time it lurches and pulls over to the curb.

"One day they're going to let pigs on buses," I say.

"I think the animal has to be small enough to sit on your lap—" Pegga says, leaning the other way. We both grin at the idea of Odin sprawled over us, like a massive sack of potatoes with a worried-pig face.

I'm heading to the library—to do my research on pot-bellies. It doesn't even bug me that Pegga calls it my "weirdo pig project."

"How is Odin going to save the earth?" Pegga asks me.

"That's what I have to find out," I say.

Pegga's coming along for the ride—which means, shopping. She loves finding silly little things at the dollar store, like butterfly barrettes or plastic straws that sing when you suck on them. But shopping bores me, whether it's with my mom, with her squeezing every fruit in the supermarket, or even with Pegga, who tries on every single hat or T-shirt, just because.

At the library, I phone home to say I'll be late, but there's no answer. Not even my dad, with his leg up, bored out of his mind. I figure maybe he's sleeping, and leave a message.

Most of the books at the library are about raising swine—which means pigs as a kind of business. I flip through the pictures of dorky-looking farmers in gumboots. Their pigs live their whole lives in huge barns with hundreds of others, numbers stapled into their ears so people can tell them apart. I can't believe they don't even have names—or mud puddles. Or plums.

I find a couple of books about pigs in ancient legends, and finally one single, rumpled one about pot-bellies as pets, and scoop them up.

Pegga's waiting for me outside Fiziks Shoes. She's prancing up and down like a circus pony, wearing a new pair of rusty-red suede sneakers.

"Nice color," I say. "Did they cost a fortune?"

"Nope—I even have money left over."

For some reason she's wearing socks on her hands, like mittens. Socks with little pink pigs circling the ankle-parts. She waves them at me.

"Here—a present," she says. "There weren't any that looked exactly like Odin."

Pegga's good at sharing. Maybe it's easier because

she's the only kid at her house and doesn't have to compete with someone like Sonja.

"Wow, thanks," I say. "That reminds me. Our next stop is the pet superstore, over in the big mall."

"I think it's a waste to be spending money on Odin, when you could be buying neat stuff for yourself," Pegga says.

"Like what?"

"Like maybe a new hoodie," she says, "or the new Smoosh CD."

A new hoodie is tempting, and I do like Smoosh— they're a two-girl band, young, like Pegga and me, and not all dolled up—and their rap songs are kind of happy. But it's not as if I have a choice. The nights are getting a little chilly for Odin's liking. I guess it's always sweaty and warm where he comes from, no freezing cold winters.

Only a few weeks ago, my mother and I could have talked about making a blanket for Odin. My mom's really good at sewing—when she has the time. But that was *before* I had to find one good reason to keep Odin.

"I have to get serious about taking care of Odin," I tell Pegga. "It's like a Survivor show at my house—and he's being voted off the island."

Even though it's getting late, Pegga and I goof

around at the pet store, talking to the angel fish and sniffing the toys stuffed with catnip. I lead Pegga around with a sequined dog collar and a leopard-skin leash, shouting out, "Sit!" "Stay!" and "Fetch!"

Pegga picks up a rubber Kong chew toy in her teeth and growls at me.

"What kind of dog are you?" I ask.

"Whoodle," she says through her snarly teeth.

"If I were a dog, I think I'd be—a sheepdog. They're really smart, and loyal, no matter what."

"Okay, now I'm a lhasa apso," Pegga says, spiking up her bangs and mussing her glossy black hair half over her face. She curls up on a giant-sized dog bed and pretends to lick her paws like some sort of pooch princess.

We're laughing ourselves silly, making bulldog faces one minute and wagging our whole bodies, like retrievers, the next.

Finally we find blankets: small knit ones for itsy-bitsy lapdogs and larger ones with tummy straps for big, hulking dogs. I try a blue-checkered one on Pegga, who's down on all fours, and try to imagine it fitting Odin. It's the wrong shape, too long, and maybe not quite chubby enough around. Pegga's making a shnarfing sound at the back of her throat that's supposed to sound like Odin.

This nerdy salesclerk asks us to stop fooling around with the merchandise.

"I'm buying this—" I tell him.

"Shnarf, shnarf, shnarf—" Pegga says, as he walks away in his dumb uniform with the dog-bone logo on the back.

The blanket's a whopping forty bucks, so I basically clean out my bank account. I even have to borrow ten dollars from Pegga.

"I'll pay you back next allowance," I promise.

On the bus home, I start to nod off with my head pressed against Odin's spiffy new blanket. The streets beyond the bus window have dark patches between the yellowish glare from the streetlights.

Pegga has to poke me in the ribs—I almost miss my stop.

"See ya," I say, shuffling off the bus.

The bus stop's right by Howard Wong's Chinese restaurant. For some reason, I decide to go in and buy everyone at home a fortune cookie. Five, including Odin.

My backpack is crammed with books and Odin's bulky blanket, sticking out the top.

"You look like a sherpa," Howard says, his round face looking hot and steamy from the kitchen.

"What's that?" I ask.

"They help people carry supplies up and down the mountains—in Tibet, in the Himalayas. They're expert climbers."

"Five fortune cookies for this sherpa, please," I say.

"That's all you want?" Howard asks, puzzled. "No egg rolls? No ginger pork?"

I make a sweet-and-sour face, and shake my head. I'm staring at a cake on his sweets counter. It has a huge, cookie-like statue of a pig on it.

"A wedding cake—" Howard says. "You wish the new couple luck with a pig. Pigs mean prosperity—" he says. "That's where the idea of piggybanks came from."

"Wow—I didn't know that."

I search around in my pockets, forgetting I don't have a nickel left. Howard sees the blank look on my face.

"Don't worry, cookies on the house," he says.

When I get home, the house is dark and silent—the back door unlocked. No sounds or smells of supper. The only telephone message is the one I left hours ago.

"Dad?"

Nobody answers.

I get a panicky feeling when I snap on the back porch light, can't see Odin anywhere in the yard. I'm about to go searching for him when I hear a car idling in the driveway. Doors slamming.

I quickly throw some knives and forks, glasses, paper napkins on the table. I set fortune cookies by everyone's placemats. I want to make a good impression—get on the right side of my mother again.

My dad limps in the door. I'm surprised to see him trying out his cane. He looks just as surprised to see me ripping up lettuce, chopping carrots, making a big mess of cutting tomatoes with a not-sharp-enough knife. My idea of salad.

My mom's right behind him with a *what next* look etched on her face. I suddenly see wrinkles around her eyes I never noticed before. Maybe after I pay Pegga back, I should save up some money to send my mother to a spa or something. Pegga's mom does that—she goes to some fancy place where they put cucumber slices on your eyes and you do yoga all day long.

It might do Sonja some good too. She winces in pain when she sees me—half her face is puffed out, and reddish, as though she's holding a hot baked potato in her cheek. I forgot—she was getting her wisdom teeth out today.

"Howard Wong showed me this neat cake today—told me that sweets in the shape of pigs are good luck in China. Could we maybe do some baking together soon, Mom?"

I expect my mother to show some interest here—she's big on my learning to cook anything beside microwave popcorn. But the subject of pigs and luck seems to hang in the air. Nobody says anything.

"Where's Odin?" I ask. "Anybody seen him?"

"Odin got into a little mishap today—" my mother says carefully, as though she's rolling each word in her mouth like a too-cold ice cube. "He could have used your help—we *all* could have. Your father had to help me shove Odin into the back of the van and take him to the vet. And your father's not supposed to be doing any heavy lifting. Odin shrieked the whole way. And he, well—left a puddle in the carpeting. Your father's not amused."

Apparently he's not talking, either. He's just sitting there, silent as a stone. Sonja's glaring at me, over her pouchy cheek.

I'm trying to blink back tears. Odin had to be scared out of his wits to actually wet himself in the car. "What happened—is he still at the vet?"

"A loose dog—well, Elvis, actually—bit Odin. In the backside. It's not as bad as he made out with all his uproar. He's probably more bruised than anything. The vet said it was fine to bring him home."

Elvis is Mrs. Trimble's dog, a leggy black-and-white mutt with a bristly coat that makes him look fierce, even though he mostly sleeps. He's so ancient, he's lived as long as I have—so, in human years he's eighty-something. Mrs. Trimble named him after Elvis Presley, because of the way he sometimes howls at night.

"Elvis and Odin were fighting over a bag of garbage in the back lane," my mother says, pursing her lips with disapproval.

"Back lane—how'd he get *there*?"

"Well—*someone* must have forgotten to latch the gate properly," my mom says with an edge to her voice.

"Well, it wasn't *me*—" I snap at her. "*I'm* not the one who takes the garbage out or goes visiting at Mrs. Trimble's." I'm remembering when my mother stomped out of the backyard in a huff, carrying her cushions.

"Tammy, that's enough," my otherwise silent father says. "You—and Odin—" He stops himself.

But there's no stopping my mother. "Your father and I have talked it over and we think it would be best for all concerned if we found Odin a new home."

"*All concerned?* What about me?" I sputter. "Plus, Odin's my project at school. I'm doing research and then a speech—" I've got that wimpy half-crying sound to my voice.

My mother gives my father a meaningful look and then says, "Well—he's got to heal first anyway. And then we'll discuss it further."

"This has NOT been a discussion," I say, quickly snapping up the fortune cookies from the table, and shoving them into my pocket.

I hear it then—a wheezing noise in the garage. I open the door from the back hall and snap on the light. Odin's hunkered down under my dad's workbench, on a pile of old car blankets and my dad's working-in-the-yard clothes, as if he couldn't wait for his cuddly new blanket. He's piled everything up and waddled around in it—like he's been painfully trying to chase his tail.

I run to him and cradle his wrinkled-up head on my knees. I sneak a peek at his wound. Teeny, tiny beads of blood are seeping to the surface of his thick skin in a horseshoe shape on his rump.

"Ouch," I say to him. "You poor thing."

Odin turns his face away, as though he's holding a grudge. He's got a point—I did kind of abandon him. He waits for me every day after school as though he's wearing a watch, and today I didn't show up.

"Come on, Odin. You know I think you're the best," I say.

We start sharing the cookies then. I figure we need as much luck as we can get.

"Yours first," I say to Odin.

I crack one open and read out: "You will have friends in high places."

Odin's eyes seem to water a little at the thought.

I slide half a cookie into my mouth, and give Odin the other piece. He really enjoys the sweet, almondy flavor—maybe it reminds him of his "home" home, back in Vietnam. He's making a slobbery mess.

"Okay, here's mine." I open the cookie slowly. "Be true to yourself and everything else will follow."

Odin smacks his lips, seems to agree.

The next two don't really cheer me up, although Odin's drooling like mad. "You have to make a decision." Big-time, I think, as Odin and I munch, munch, munch. And then, "Home is where the heart is."

I gently break open the last one. "Family are best friends." Yeah, right.

I'm holding the last cookie in my hand—my stomach growling like crazy. I look through the half-open door into the house, toward the kitchen. I can see hunched figures at the table eating dinner. I decide to wait until the coast is clear, then I'll sneak something from the fridge to my bedroom.

Odin grunts impatiently, as if to say it's his turn. Suddenly he tilts his head and clamps down on my hand, snatching the cookie.

"Ow! Odin, that really hurt—mind your manners."

I'm shaking my hand, trying to make Odin feel sorry. But Odin turns up his chin and pulls himself to a sitting position, his sore hip off to one side. He snorts once, and looks off into the distance.

Great. Now even Odin is turning against me.

5

Movie Mania

Odin's omniverous. That means he can eat almost anything, from meat or vegetables to fancy flowers or junk food, just like people do. That's what it says in one of my library books, called *Keeping Pot-bellies*.

It describes the right way to feed pigs treats: while facing them, because otherwise they take sideways swipes at things they can't quite see or reach. It also mentions a pig's sharpest teeth, the tusk-like ones, and how they can do a lot of damage. No kidding.

The next morning, three fingers on my right hand are so swollen I can't even make a fist. At the breakfast table, I keep my hand down in my lap, out of sight. I'm eating cereal like a total klutz with my left, flipping through the pot-bellies book with my spoon. Between bites I learn that Odin's distant relatives chow down on sweet potatoes and water hyacinth.

Yawning Sonja has gone back to bed—she's resting up after having her teeth yanked. My mom's working some crazy night shift, so I'm keeping the silent man behind the newspaper company.

"How's it going, Pop-sicle?" I ask him.

He usually says, "I scream, you scream, we all scream for ice cream" in reply. It's our corny way of saying hello. Or used to be, when he was still his normal, joking self. But this morning there's an awkward silence.

"Did you know there are 13 million pigs in Vietnam? That's more pigs per family than TVs or cars, or anything we have oodles of here."

His newspaper stays up over his face. Maybe he didn't hear me.

"How big IS Vietnam, anyway?"

"About twice as big as Florida, I suppose," he says, in a tired, creaky voice. "Or half as big as France. Maybe you should look in an atlas."

He's trying. But for some reason I have this horrible feeling he's in on my mother's plot to have Odin REMOVED.

I scribble a left-handed SWEET POTATOES on my mom's grocery list. It's a long shot, like a losing lottery ticket for Odin. But I figure it can't hurt. I've been doing things like that lately, keeping my fingers crossed for good luck. Well, the ones I can still cross.

I find myself walking to school in the middle of the

road. I'm playing a kind of kooky game in my head: if the cars whizzing past miss me, I'll be able to keep Odin, no matter what. I keep chanting: *Vietnam is half of France, I am Odin's big, fat chance, Vietnam is half of France, I am Odin's big, fat chance . . .* I try to imagine relocating Odin to a place that's not my backyard. Florida's warmer than Canada's west coast, more steamy and stormy like the weather in Vietnam. But if dottery old Elvis could sneak up on Odin, alligators would terrify him, give him nightmares about being gobbled up.

I consider sending him to France. Maybe he could earn his keep finding truffles. They're like rare mushrooms—you have to go poking around in forests to find them, and people actually use pigs to sniff them out. But when I think about him stuck in some farmy pigpen except for rare outings, and everyone shouting "Bonjour!" all day long, I panic, get all sweaty on my forehead. The sounds of traffic drift farther and farther away.

A few cars go around me really slowly, to see whether I'm all right. Another driver honks because he thinks I'm some sort of nutbar or super-brat. But I stay there, wandering down the center line—it's as though it's not even me in my hoodie and scruffy jeans, but someone else.

"Get off the street, you idiot!" someone shouts.

I look around, startled, and point at myself, as in, *Do you mean me?*

The man's leaning out of his car window so far, he's practically upside down.

"Yes, you—who do you think?"

So I snap out of it. Trudge all the rest of the way to school on the sidewalk.

We're sitting in assembly, practically the whole school crammed into the gym. The grade eights are packed together like sardines in the bleachers, and the grade nines get the good seats in the front, closer to the stage, because they're supposed to sit more quietly, I guess. Except they're acting up, being loud and hyper, laughing at nothing at all and scraping their chairs around.

We're supposed to be getting some "special guest" from Voodoo Studios. Everyone is kind of excited and goosebumpy. I don't get the whole fame thing, I guess, because all I'm feeling is hot and sticky, as though there isn't enough air for hundreds of kids.

When the film hotshot finally shows up twenty minutes late, he's wearing a black shirt and a string tie with a silver bronco hanging down his chest. He has a skimpy little ponytail that looks ridiculous. I mean, the tassle on the end of Odin's tail is bigger.

And suddenly—just thinking about Odin's tail, I'm feeling dizzy.

The gym walls close in on me, and all I can feel is my

sore fingers throb-throb-throbbing like crazy. I realize how Odin's bite is just one more point for my mom. Against Odin, against me. I mean, we're keeping score now—happy or not, Odin or not.

Pegga can see I'm all shaky. "Are you all right, Tammy? Are you feeling sick? Is it your crunched hand? It looks super-red—and sort of blotchy."

I give her a dirty look. I told her not to make a big deal out of my Odin-bite and I wish she wouldn't.

She puts her hand in the middle of my back, between my shoulder blades. Then says, "Here, breathe into your back—slowly."

It's something Pegga's mom teaches in her yoga class. I try to concentrate, but everything good and bad that's ever happened to Odin keeps whirling through my head. When I finally do breathe more deeply, she says, "Yup, that's it. Now again."

I have to admit it's really neat: like a dark chocolate breath, slow and delicious. Everything swims back into focus again, the colored lines painted on the glossy floors, the stage with its purple curtains, the crowd of eager faces. Including Pegga's, beside me.

"What's with this celebrity's black pointy cowboy boots?" I whisper to her. "What does he do—mainly westerns or something?"

"Shhh," Pegga says. "I want to hear what he says."

Danny Dynasty—he swears that's his real name—is

a locations manager. He finds places to make movies that "could be anywhere." Like a beach on the Pacific Ocean that looks as though it could be the Atlantic. Or the Mediterranean. I haven't seen enough beaches or oceans to know the difference.

"A few years ago," Danny brags, "we made an epic film about samurai warriors in Japan. Except the whole thing was shot in the foothills in Alberta."

Everyone ooohs and aaahs and laughs just the right amount. Danny likes all the attention, you can tell. He laughs at his own jokes before he even tells them.

Some of the stuff he tells us is interesting, though. Like fake Styrofoam rocks looking more real on film than actual boulders. It's safer to use pretend stone, and easier to move back into place after filming explosions or disasters.

Danny describes a Christmas movie he recently "wrapped"—which means finished—that had skaters twirling around on some high-tech material called Glice; it's like all-weather ice so it doesn't need to be freezing outside to shoot a winter scene.

"So we're being tricked every time we look at a movie screen," Walter Cluster says to Mr. Dynasty in the question period afterward.

"Basically, yes," Mr. Voodoo Studios says. He's even kind of pleased that someone pointed it out.

He and Walter have a long chat, as Walter describes it

later. Walter's so excited, he acts as though he's about to burst onto the scene as a nerd-kid movie director. He's got this idea to make a Halloween horror movie, he tells us. I roll my eyes at him, in real horror.

"Like suddenly Walter Cluster's a filmmaker," I scoff to Pegga after he trots off.

"Listen, I don't think it's a bad idea," Pegga says. "I think I'll try to get a part acting in his film—I mean, if the script isn't totally embarrassing. It might be fun."

"Walter Cluster's the director," I remind her.

She shrugs and grabs my hand—my sore one. "Come on—let's go to my place and practice crying on cue. It's supposed to be really hard to do."

I pull my hand back. A shockwave of pain keeps tingling in my fingers.

"I thought they put drops in their eyes, to make it look like real tears," I say.

"No way—good actresses train themselves to feel a sad emotion, and then they break into sobs, I swear—"

"Listen, I have to get home. I don't want the three grumps at my house to have to deal with Odin." I realize I sound a little cranky myself.

"That's too bad," Pegga says. She pulls down her mouth as if she's trying to find the right film star face to be sympathetic.

"Can't you practice crying at my house?" I suggest. "It'd be easy. Everyone's always in a bad mood."

"Well—don't take this personally, okay? But I don't really feel like babysitting Odin."

"Suit yourself," I say.

In one way I don't blame her for not wanting to come over. My mom was such a pain about the stupid sofa cushions. But I also think Pegga could be helping me figure out a good way to keep Odin. Not worrying about becoming a grade eight actress.

"Don't forget about tomorrow," I remind her, just in case she spends the whole evening swooning.

"What's to forget?"

"Rough outlines for our speeches—for Diana."

"Oh, I've already done mine," Pegga says. "I got all this stuff out of a yoga magazine—how if you stay calm, and eat less meat, and help others stay healthy, it's not only good for you but for the entire earth . . . It's a big-picture thing. Look, this is my favorite pose—Tree Pose."

She stands on one leg, pointing her arms straight up, palms pressed together, as if she's some kind of girl-arrow. "Can you feel my energy touching the sky and sinking deep into the ground? It's just like a tree must feel."

Just looking at Pegga trying to keep from tipping is making me dizzy again.

"Well—I've been putting my project off, I guess. It seems pointless somehow—to learn about pigs just so someone else can take care of Odin one day. And don't you dare say anything about Odin, you know—nipping me. Then my mother would really be on my case to turf him out—"

"Shnarf, shnarf," Pegga says, cutting me off.

She smiles at me like we're still the best of friends. But I'm not too sure.

Nurse Tammy

Odin's in the garage, feeling a little sore after his escapade. Or maybe it's sorry for himself. The funny thing is—he looks bigger than his usual shape. Puffed up, as if he's swallowed a bunch of helium or something. He gives out a long-winded sigh, then whimpers a little. Makes a little-kid-with-a-tummy-ache sound I've never heard before. Holds his belly in—as if he's holding his breath—then pushes it out again. Hardly lifts up his head to squint at me.

I dash back into the house, grab my library books. Plunk myself back down beside Mr. Flat-out Odin. I skim the list of symptoms. It sounds a lot like a person's checklist of being sick. No appetite, not wanting to get out of bed, all curled up in pain.

One book says that pigs like music; a piggery in Mexico used to hire boys whose only job was to sing to the animals. What a great after-school job, I think. Better than flinging papers or fast food.

I turn on my dad's radio—it starts playing a lame country song. Odin groans some more. I don't blame him. I scan a few other stations—find a little classical stuff, with violins squeaking out high notes. Odin gives me another helpless look. I finally decide on STAR FM—the oldies station. I actually like some of the stuff they play, like the Beatles.

Odin twitches his tail a little to some song called "Hotel California." Meanwhile, I'm trying to count how many times a minute he's breathing. I guess you start breathing faster and faster if you're in a lot of pain. I learned that from my mom—so it can't be that different for pigs.

I count watching Odin's fat flank—he's supposed to be breathing twenty to thirty times per minute, and he's at thirty-five. Not too bad. But I have no idea how to find his pulse. In movies, people are always finding an artery in your neck or something. Fat chance—Odin's neck is like a sumo wrestler's, except with more flab, less muscle.

Once I saw my mom helping this woman who'd fainted over her shopping cart at the supermarket. Mom kept pressing her first two fingers over the woman's wrist. So I find a little pitter-patter just above Odin's hoof—

In the summer, when Sam first got Odin, his hooves were way too long, curling up at the toes. It was actually painful for him to walk. So Sam and a couple of his friends had to puppy-pile on top of Odin while some farm vet did a house call. He used hoof cutters that looked like giant toenail clippers. Odin shrieked his head off, and one of Sam's neighbors came over to see what was getting butchered, as he put it.

I lose count of Odin's heartbeats and have to start over again. One hundred and one—and it's supposed to be 70 to 110 beats a minute. So he's not close to dying yet.

He lets out this terrible wheezing sound and tries to stand up. He's only halfway to his feet when all this yellow-looking slop comes out of his mouth, with black rubbery bits in it.

"Looks like he swallowed an old boot," my dad says. He's morphed out of nowhere, and is standing in the doorway to the house, leaning crookedly on his cane.

And then I remember. Elvis. The back lane.

"He must have gobbled up something in the garbage yesterday—" I say, wrinkling up my nose.

"And it took this long to hit stomach central," my dad agrees.

Odin's convulsing a little, like the dry heaves.

I have to give my dad brownie points. He actually

holds open the plastic bag while I clean up Odin's barf, heave the sopping paper towels. And he *doesn't* notice that I'm mainly using my left hand.

Odin is suddenly fast asleep and snoring.

"Well, he looks a little less miserable now," my dad says. "Supper's almost ready," he adds.

"Great," I say, my stomach still churning. "I'll have to work up an appetite—But hey, Dad, thanks for the help."

At supper nobody says anything about the night before, but you can tell everyone's thinking about it. They're almost trying to be cheerful or something. But it's not quite working. Everyone's still on edge, prickly.

My mother's whipping around the kitchen as though she's making supper in a fire drill: march one, two, three, and out the door. Even though she has tonight off, it's like she's stuck in some work-work-work groove.

"I took Odin's vitals today. You know, just for practice," I say, trying to get her attention on a subject we can share.

I give my dad a keep-this-to-yourself look when he opens his mouth to say something about Odin's queasy stomach. My dad turns whatever he was going to say into a yawn.

"Hmm? What was that, Tammy?"

"His vital signs, like breathing and his pulse—"

"Going to become a vet now, are you?" my mom asks, still clattering around the kitchen in a frenzy. "Your marks would have to be top-notch, you know."

I ignore the part about my marks.

Sonja gives me an I-told-you-so half-grin with one side of her face while she sips on her chicken-noodle soup. She's having it lukewarm—the way Odin likes it—because otherwise it hurts too much. The rest of us are having fish and chips, usually one of my favorites, especially my mom's homemade fries. But I'm just toying with my food.

I'm wondering if Odin's only a little sick, or maybe dying. Maybe he only looked like he was sleeping, and now he's barely clinging to life.

"I think Odin's just malingering," my mother says, right out of the blue, when she finally plunks herself down in her chair. It's as though she's reading my mind—she's always been good at that. And she's used that expression before, so I know exactly what it means.

"Why would an animal fake being sick?" I ask. I'm almost insulted on Odin's behalf—after all he's been through. "It's not as if Odin's trying to stay home from school and watch reruns of *Star Trek*."

"Maybe so he could hang around this comfy house a little longer," my mom says, her fork stopped halfway to her open mouth. "Maybe the next thing I know, he'll want me to make *him* some homemade chicken soup. Or buy him ice cream or ginger ale."

I can't tell if she's joking or not. I want to insist that Odin really *is* sick, that he barfed up a lung. That it's all Elvis's fault. Or hers. But I don't.

Instead I hear a girl's voice that sounds just like mine offering to give up my allowance for the next couple of months, just to help pay for Odin's expenses. I even hear the Tammy-voice offer to do extra vacuuming and clean up my room. It's like I can't help myself, once I get started.

My mother asks me then if I'm going to be doing all this tidying with only my left hand. She's watching me eat, my right shoulder slumped down, my hand with the fat, sausage-fingers tucked away in my lap.

"I'm trying to break old habits," I say carefully. "It's this game we're playing—a bunch of us at school."

"Oh, we used to do that too," my mom says, actually smiling at me. "We had Left-Hand Days. At lunch we ate with our lefts and after school we played hopeless field hockey or softball—because in class, even if you were naturally left-handed, you were only allowed to use your right hand. So it was a kind of rebellion, I suppose."

I'm surprised to hear about my mom being any kind of a rebel. But I'm also dying to change the subject. So I tell everyone about Danny Dynasty. How he thought he was too cool for our school, and I thought he was a dork.

"I know what you mean," my dad says. "These film people think they're so great, and they're everywhere these days. No wonder it's hard to find parking downtown; there's always a line of movie trailers, and security people telling you to move along. Just this summer I heard someone with a megaphone telling me to 'walk normally.' Can you imagine? All I was doing was shuffling down the sidewalk with a crowd of other people. How was I to know they were movie extras?"

I guess my dad told the hotshot director he had a right to walk down the street any way he wanted. We all laugh—even Sonja, with a painful, crooked grin.

And then, thank goodness, the phone rings. My dad reaches for it before I can get there. We pretend to struggle for it.

"It's your old boyfriend from grade five," my dad says, keeping the receiver out of my lefty reach. "Willy What's-his-name—"

"It's your old girlfriend from high school," I say. "The one with the buck teeth."

My mom's actually grinning her face off, just watching us. And Sonja too, although it hurts to smile, so she's holding the side of her face and groaning at the same time. It's almost like a normal mood at our house. The way it used to be.

"Tammy—it's for you," my father says in this mock-serious voice when he finally hands the receiver to me. "It's Sam."

I'm confused. A million things go through my head. Maybe my parents have asked Sam to take Odin back. They'd never stoop to that . . . Or would they?

Or maybe Sam's phoned to see how Sonja is.

But Sam says, "Hey, Tammy, you're just who I wanted to talk to."

"I am?"

"I want to know whether you and Odin can do me a favor. We're having a garage sale—for Pet Safe. Do you know about them? They're this group that saves mistreated animals. And I have to be at a swim meet on Saturday. So I thought you might have fun sitting there with Odin—it's going to be outside, at the Valleyfair Mall. I've already cleared it with Mrs. Bing; she's the one in charge. You can take my place—put on price stickers, put things in bags for customers, collect money. What do you say?"

I'm thinking a lot of things at the same time. Like, wow, what a lifesaver. How neat Sam is to have thought of me. I'm also thinking, *"My right hand's aching like crazy, and Odin's in rough shape, probably too*

nervous to leave the property, liable to snap at people like an
ancient snapping turtle . . ."

Still, I say, "Hey, sure! Why not?"

Then Sam says, "By the way, is Sonja there? How's
she feeling?"

I look in Sonja's direction. Part of me wants to be
mean, but she looks so pathetic trying to sip ginger ale
out of a straw. She has a bit of noodle stuck on her
lower lip.

"Still pretty sore, I guess. Her face is all swollen. I
don't know if she can talk to you."

Sonja doesn't look up. She's listening, though.

"Just say hi to her then, okay?" Sam has this soft,
coaxing sound to his voice, like saying hi to Sonja
means more in the world to him than anything.

So that's why he really called, I think. I feel a little
disappointed.

My mom's hovering. "What did Sam want?" she asks.

"He de-sss-perately needs me to fill in for him—for a
Pet Safe sale," I say. "With Odin," I add quickly.

I'm thinking it might be the fourth good reason to
keep Odin. Composter, ace school project, the world's
heaviest good luck charm, and now Odin as volunteer.
An "all-round good sort of chap," as my mom might
say. That is, if she liked Odin one little bit.

"He also wanted to know how Sonja's doing. He says
hi. Hopes she's feeling better soon."

I look straight at puffy-faced Sonja. I can see a lot of

different emotions flicker in her eyes. She looks relieved, then confused, then angry as can be. And right after, she looks as though she'd crack a happy smile if she could.

I actually feel sorry for her. I've missed Sam too.

Liar, Liar

It doesn't seem as if I've slept at all when the alarm goes off at six. I basically spent the whole night checking on Odin. My eyes feel too scratchy to open.

"We're out of Pepto Dismal," I mutter. That's what I used to call it when I was a little kid, so it became a family joke.

Last night I poured a lot of the chalky pink stuff into Odin's snout. He didn't seem to mind the fake cherry taste. At one point I dozed off in the garage, next to him, and remember practically sleepwalking back through the living room. Everyone else was still up, but no one seemed to see me. There was some show on TV about redecorating cluttered kitchens, Sonja was flipping through one of her magazines, and my dad was nodding off, his eyes glazed. My mom was knitting something for Christmas—she was click-clicking with her needles right in front of the people bound to be getting the wooly thing bunched in her lap.

I hit the snooze button and fall asleep again, thinking about a long, long scarf in a dingy brown, with green and yellow bits in it. I'm hoping it wasn't a barf-scarf for me.

I wake up for the zillionth time. It's still dark outside my window—and raining. I can hear cars going swish, swish on the roads. It's weird that so many people are going to work while I'm usually sleeping.

I click on the bedside lamp. My right hand has turned into a monster paw; the whole hand's swollen now, with creases in it from being pressed under my pillow. The funny thing is, it's not as sore. More numb, like it doesn't belong to me anymore.

I put a big book across my lap and write on a sheet of paper: *"Pot-bellies make the world go round."*

All this stuff I didn't even know I knew comes pouring out. It's as if I was working on it in my twitchy sleep. My left-handed writing's not bad—a little back-slanted, but readable.

Pot-bellies in Viet Nam are treated like children. They're fed at the table with scraps and washed in the bathwater, after the kids. They help warm the house, and are perfect composters for garbage. Their manure makes the rice paddies grow, and then they eat the rice waste.

In the Mekong Delta or Red River regions, pot-bellies live on bamboo rafts planted with sweet potatoes. People collect water snails for the pigs, and cook them just right, as if they're in a posh French restaurant. The pigs leave their droppings in the water, and that helps the water plants grow that feed the fish. Then people eat the sweet potatoes and fish, and share the leftovers with the pigs. It's an amazing cycle where nothing gets wasted.

The only bad part is that people end up eating the family pig. He's kind of a best friend, and then suddenly he's lunch. I don't really get that part—it would be so hard after you knew a pig personally. After you gave him a name, and got to know his fave foods and tickle spots.

In Odin's case, it's grapes, and cabbage, just slightly cooked, when my mom's making cabbage rolls. And he likes me to rub a spot between his front legs, or under his chin, with just the right pressure. Then he leans a little into my hand.

In Viet Nam a pig roast is a traditional way to celebrate. Especially at religious festivals or weddings. Lard from the pigs makes candles for light in all the houses without electricity. So sometimes pigs are more useful dead than alive.

I guess with 13 million pigs in Viet Nam, there have to be pigs going to market sooner or later. Then a family has to get another good pig—and start all over again. Raising litters of piglets.

I looked in an atlas to see how big Viet Nam is. But it's hard to tell, because all the countries are on different pages, and some maps zoom in on certain places like they're important, and leave others as small blobs.

That's as far as I get before my hand starts cramping.

The outline takes about two minutes to read aloud—I time myself. With a few more details, I figure it's almost a whole speech. It has that conversational style Diana wanted—to make it interesting for people who might not be big fans of pot-bellied pigs.

But all at once everything I've learned about Odin's relatives starts to depress me. Pot-bellies do so much in Viet Nam, yet they're so helpless. They're part of a family for years, and then suddenly—they're not.

It's Free Friday. Which, in Miss Pickle's class, means we get to choose some special treat while we work. It can be music in the background—not too loud—or a food treat. Cookies from home, or popcorn, shared with everyone. Things like that. And she gets something special too. It's kind of a break for all of us. Puts us on an equal footing, as Miss Pickles says.

This week she's having a pot of tea at her desk while she reads our outlines; we can hear her sip-sipping happily. Now and then she smiles or scribbles a note in the margin. She's going to be talking to us one at a time to give us pointers about our speeches.

And today we get to chew gum, even blow huge bubbles, just as long as we throw it all out later in the wastebasket. Not stick it to the desks or anything. And who would? That would only ruin Free Fridays for the rest of the year.

That's what I like about Miss Pickles. She thinks of us as more than just silly students to be bossed around and marked as either smart or not so smart.

Today's project is an example. It's a new policy, she tells us, for each student to have a survival kit in case of an earthquake. It's a distinct possibility, I guess, with our old brick school and all the crummy portables plunked on a fault line, a big crack under the earth's surface that runs all the way up the coast from California to Alaska.

This year Diana's in charge of the grade eight kits. It could be a whole day or even two, she reminds us, until we could make contact with friends or family, if a serious shake-up happened during school hours. So we need to bring juice boxes, a few granola bars, and a fleecy blanket. The emergency supplies get stored in a small cement building separate from the actual school. Just in case, she says.

"Just in case the whole school falls to rubble," Walter Cluster exclaims, as though he's fascinated by the idea.

Diana ignores him. "Along with your food snacks you are also asked to bring a family photo and a comfort letter."

"What's a comfort letter?" Pegga asks.

"Well, the younger grades are getting notes written by their parents or other family members. But I think you're old enough to create your own letters. Let's face it, by the time a student is in grade eight, parents might not know exactly what makes their children happy—they're growing up."

"Hear, hear," Walter Cluster says.

"Shut up, Walter Cluster," a bunch of us mutter aloud. It sounds like none of us is grown-up at all.

"So—" Miss Pickles continues, "I want you to think what kinds of things might comfort you in a time of crisis. You might bring a family photo—or one of a friend. And for your letters, some of you may want to write down the lyrics of a song that makes you feel good, or you might want a close pal, someone special, to write something that cheers you up. I'm entrusting each of you to put some thought into this."

Missy Miles sticks her skinny arm up and waves it

around. "Can we bring a stuffed animal? Figure skaters use them for good luck."

We all gawk at Missy. Even though lots of us still sleep with stuffies on our beds just like little kids, she's the only one stupid enough to admit it out loud.

People put their heads down, start to scribble. We're all chewing gum like crazy, as if our lives depend on it. It's as if Miss Pickles knows just how to treat us to get us eager to do something.

I haven't the slightest idea where I could drum up any sort of feel-good letter. Maybe a sarcastic postcard from Sonja? Or how about a new threat from my mother?

Dear Tammy:

I took the time during the earthquake to take Odin back to that smelly old pet shop. I just couldn't cope, what with the dining room ceiling caved in and everything.

Love and kisses, your mother.

Right. All I can wonder is who *would* take care of Odin if I was stuck at school in any kind of disaster. Who'd be giving *him* juice boxes and granola bars?

And then I think, Sam, that's who. So maybe I should write a pretend will, giving Odin back to Sam, in case my school falls to dust and I can't get home. Or wait, maybe Sam should write me official permission to take care of Odin . . . no matter what. That would make me feel better, lots better.

I start to write, almost automatically now, with my left hand:

Dear Cammy:
In the event of an earthquake, there's no one I trust to take better care of Odin.
Even if everything starts shaking and quaking, and his trough behind the house becomes a huge mudslide, I want you to move him to a safe place. Never let him out of your sight. You're the best person I can think of to comfort Odin.

I can't quite figure out how Sam would sign this letter. Your friend? Odin's pal?

It doesn't really matter anyway. I could never show it to Sam. I'd be too shy. Too *mortified*, as Pegga might say. Sam would only wonder what was up. And I never, ever want Sam to know I might not have enough good reasons to keep Odin.

Comfort schmomfort, I think.

At the end of class, Miss Pickles calls me up to her desk. She thinks my outline looks fascinating, although she reminds me that Vietnam is one word, not two.

Minor detail, I think. Spelling is the least of my worries. A lot of smart people are terrible spellers—it's almost a sure sign you're going to become an inventor or a great musician.

Miss Pickles tells me I only needed to do the outline in point form. She thinks I'm quite a good writer, though. In the class presentation, she'd like to hear a few more facts about pigs like Odin, about their habits, or why they have pot-bellies.

"Sure," I say. "I'm learning more every day."

And every night too. I have to stifle a yawn when I remember Odin's tummy upset, and how little sleep I got.

"You haven't forgotten you offered to go first? Right after Thanksgiving?"

"Oh, I haven't forgotten," I say.

Miss Pickles tilts her head a little, as if she's curious about something.

"Aren't you right-handed, Tammy?"

I look at her blankly and get red in the face. I guess she was watching me write my make-believe comfort letter. For some reason I can't think of anything sensible to say. Her blue eyes seem to be looking right through me.

"Well, a dog—our neighbor's dog—bit me," I blurt out. "He was bullying Odin, my pig—and I had to protect him." My face is more flushed than ever.

"Let me see it—" Miss Pickles says, her voice concerned.

I pull out my fat flipper of a right hand. She gives a mini-gasp.

"Have you had a tetanus shot?" she asks. "When did this happen?"

"Yesterday? Or maybe—the day before," I mumble, frantic to say one thing that isn't an outright lie.

"Well, you have to go to the health unit after school. I'll write a note to your parents—"

I sway a little on my feet, heat flaring up the back of my neck.

"Are you feeling feverish?" Diana asks. "I don't mind driving you—I go right past the clinic—"

"Do you have to—send the note?" I stammer.

"Tammy, don't your parents know about this?" Miss Pickles asks sternly. One of her red sketched-in eyebrows shoots up.

"Not exactly," I say.

And that's when I act like a total idiot and tell her everything, even about Sonja wanting Odin to become a roast with a stewed apple stuck in his mouth. And about Sam and Sonja being all lovey-dovey and Odin being a big, fat friendship ring, and then there being no friendship. And about my parents freaking out about every little thing Odin does, even though they should know he's like a four-year-old human—that's what it said in one of my books—and not bound to grow up anytime soon. And that's exactly why he's so odd, and goofy, and forgivable, 'cause he's just like a little kid. With likes and dislikes, and things that scare him silly.

The only thing I don't tell her is that this "little kid"—Odin—is the one who bit me.

"Last night—" I start to say; I've been talking so fast I feel out of breath, "it was almost getting better at our house, so I don't really want—"

"I'm sorry, Tammy," Miss Pickles says. I can see she means it. "I *have* to tell your parents about the injection. And you *need* a tetanus shot—I can't change that."

I watch Diana write the note in her perfect loopy handwriting. And yes, it says "dog bite" as clear as can be. There's no mistaking it for anything else, not even "pig bite." Which would be worse, even though it's the truth.

Diana puts the note in an envelope and seals it, writes in the upper left-hand corner:

Miss Diana Pickles.

And right smack in the center:

Attention: Mr.& Mrs. Gifford

I, Tammy Rose Gifford, am toast.

8

Hot Water

I'm learning that when things are bad, you can always make them worse.

Miss Pickles not only drives me to the clinic but waits for me outside—sits in the garden on a bench. She says she needs some fresh air. I have a hunch she's scared of needles, and can't stand to watch me get the shot. But the trick is to close your eyes and grind your teeth a little and then it doesn't hurt at all.

I don't share this little tidbit with Miss Pickles, though. She looks relieved when I come out, and insists on dropping me at home in case I'm feeling feverish or incapacitated, as she puts it.

My temperature *does* rise when we pass a whole bunch of kids, including Pegga. Everyone stares at me in Miss Pickles' car, like they can't decide whether I'm some sort of teacher's pet or someone in trouble.

Bingo. *In trouble*—that's me. And getting in deeper

all the time. Luckily, my dad's not watching at the front window when Diana drops me off.

I hustle inside and go straight to my room. I take the letter from **Miss Diana Pickles** and stuff it into my clothes hamper.

I hear a harumphing sound by the back step. Odin. He's covered with mud, red and yellow leaves pasted to him like some sort of pig collage. And he's clearly hungry. I feed him some pellets to make up for the meals he missed yesterday. He tilts his head up and makes a happy face at me, his lips crinkling in a smile.

"Things are looking up," I say to him. Now I'm lying even to Odin.

I slide on his harness; it has fleece inside the straps so it won't rub his shoulders, and luckily it's nowhere near the sore spot on his hip. Although the Elvis nip looks like it's healing.

"How about a walk to the corner mailbox, buddy?"

We saunter down the sidewalk, Odin snorting and snuffling, pulling toward every cast-off candy wrapper along the way. It makes me realize just how much garbage there is floating around.

At one point Odin whirls around and practically knocks me flying. I guess he smells the dog even before I catch sight of it—a Doberman up on its toes, straining on its leash.

"Hey, chill there, buddy," I say, scratching Odin under the chin. "It's okay—I won't let him near you."

Odin presses his body against the back of my knees—I can feel him trembling. We take a shortcut through the flowerbeds of Pleasantview, the nursing home, where Odin snaps off a few late-blooming marigolds, and squats behind the bushes for a bathroom break.

This is fun, I think. Lately I've slipped a bit with my Odin duties, what with school and my hand puffing up. I need to take him out for walks more often. He was getting used to cars whooshing past and shapes hovering above him, things like window-washers and cranes on construction sites. Now, since his scuffle with Elvis, he's back to scurrying away when any kind of shadow looms, even big crows on telephone lines.

We're almost home when a black cat comes scuttling out from behind a hedge. A small, teenage-looking cat, just past kitten. I think Odin's going to wig out, but instead he sniffs the cat and it rubs up against him. The cat purrs and Odin makes chuff-chuff-chuff noises of happy-to-see-you-too; it's as if they're long-lost friends, they're so cuddly.

"You never know who your friends are," I say.

Just then a car slows down on the street and putters along right beside us. A long car shadow sweeps over the sidewalk and Odin starts to look anxious. Suddenly I hear a familiar voice.

"It's just like Danny Dynasty said—this could be anywhere!"

Definitely Walter Cluster. I swing my head toward the car and frown.

"Is that Odin?" Walter shouts, from the back seat. The window's rolled down and he's pointing a camcorder right at Odin.

"No, it's my *other* pig," I say.

I squint to see who's driving. It looks like an older version of Walter Cluster—his brother, maybe. Same overbite and weird hairline—kind of pointy in the middle of his forehead. Walter's maybe-brother has a goofy smile on his face, like he's the happiest chauffeur alive.

"We were just cruising around, trying to find you," Walter says. "And then—*Voila*! Which is French for *there you are!* With a black cat too—which is so edddgy."

Sitting right beside Walter is Pegga, laughing her head off as though he's hilarious.

"I phoned—" Pegga says, "but no one knew where you were. And I said, that's strange, 'cause you got a ride home with Miss Pickles ages ago—"

"You said what?!" If I didn't have Odin on a leash, I would reach inside the car and strangle Pegga with my one good hand. How *could* she?

"I mean, I didn't know if you were sick or something," she says. "You know—with your munched fingers?"

I glare at Pegga. If she mentioned Odin chomping my hand to my parents, I'll never speak to her again.

"That's good, verrrry edgy," says Walter, who's still

pointing the camera, first at my glowering face, and then at my feet, where Odin's getting himself all tangled up in the leash.

"Stop pointing that thing at me!" I snap at Walter.

"Why—is Odin having a bad hair day?" More giggles from the car.

"Hey listen, late afternoon light is everything," Walter says. "And Odin's very . . . photogenic."

"And edgy . . ." someone squished next to Pegga in the back seat says. Everyone laughs again.

What's with this new word, *edgy*? And what's with the hyper laughs?

I turn away and walk quickly down the sidewalk, practically dragging Odin along behind me. I'm so mad at blabbermouth Pegga I can hardly think straight.

When Odin realizes he's almost home, he starts to trot a little, his belly swinging from side to side. Let the ditzy film crew take their stupid pictures, I think, as the car slowly slides by and up the street, honking goodbye.

In a way, Walter's right—this *could* be anywhere. Our ho-hum rancher on a street with a lot of others looking almost exactly the same.

Except Odin doesn't think so. He's making a beeline for our front gate, looking relieved to be turning in at 1411 Plumtree Place. This is his home now. *This* is where he wants to be.

I, personally, would rather be at some other address.

I'm sitting at the supper table with a thermometer in my mouth, and dunking my right hand in a bowl of steaming salt water so hot it's bringing tears to my eyes.

"An old cure," my mother says, "before there were antibiotics like penicillin."

My mother is *not impressed*. She repeats that at least five times during her lecture on lockjaw. She reminds me that Odin is a barnyard animal who spends a lot of time in the dirt. Where nasty germs and bacteria grow. I can see where this is heading; now he's a risk to my health.

"I thought it was getting better," I say feebly, almost crunching the thermometer between my teeth.

My mother turns to my dad then, as if I'm invisible, and informs him that Miss Pickles is certainly a special teacher.

"How many others would not only drive a child home," she asks him, "but also phone later and check on the so-called 'dog bite'?"

So I guess it wasn't Pegga who blew my cover. Which is too bad because I slammed the phone down on her this afternoon. First I called her all sorts of names for getting me into trouble. Why did she have to be *so PATHETIC, such a snitch-witch? What kind of a friend was she, anyway?* I really blew off steam.

For a while it made me feel better. But now, on top of everything else, I owe Pegga an apology.

"Tetanus is not something you *wait* to have happen," my mother continues.

I can tell she's just getting warmed up.

"People used to die of it. Your muscles would seize up, like someone stuck in a deep freeze. You couldn't talk and you couldn't even swallow—that's why it was called lockjaw."

I get it already, Mom, I want to say.

"Tammy, what were you *thinking*?"

She seems to be waiting for a reply. I point at the thermometer and moan.

"I mean, to make up some story about Elvis biting you. You know, that pig's become more than a nuisance. He's—"

I spit the thermometer out, and hand it coldly to my mother. "It *is* Elvis's fault; he's the one that bit Odin. And then Odin bit me because he was afraid—and in pain." I don't mention that Odin was also being greedy for fortune cookies.

My mother is grinding her voice to a point, like a pencil being sharpened. "I'm not talking about the bite, Tammy. I'm talking about your lying: you hiding Miss Pickles' letter and covering up the truth—"

"What choice do I *have* with everyone always picking on Odin?" I blurt out. "Odin *this* and Odin *that*—like everything in the world is *his* fault—"

"I'm not going to argue about this," my mother says in that same pointy-pencil voice. "Odin's not leaving the yard and you're not leaving the house. You're both grounded."

"But tomorrow's Saturday! And I promised Sam I'd be at the Pet Safe sale!" I shriek. "I promised! *We promised!* I have to take Odin—"

Suddenly I clam up. My mother's face is unmoving, rigid, as though she's the one coming down with lockjaw. And Sonja's staring at me like I'm some sort of alien who doesn't know the rules for living on earth. Worst of all, my dad's chewing on his lower lip. He only does that when he's stewing, good and mad about something.

I guess I'm the something.

Then the phone rings. I sprint toward it. It might be Miss Pickles, calling to have another chat with my mother, maybe about the personal stuff I blabbed about our family falling apart at the seams. Or maybe it's Sam, making sure I'll show up for the garage sale. I'm still planning to go, no matter what my mom says. But I don't want her to hear me saying so.

I feel jumpy and nervous. It's like my whole life is one big stretching of the truth, one secret leading to another, with Odin the only one who won't tell a soul.

At least I'm reaching for the phone with my right hand; I can actually curl my fingers around the receiver. So boiling my hand to a pulp must work.

Which is a good thing, because my left arm's hot and tender from the tetanus shot.

There's a silence when I say hello.

"Pegga?" I ask.

Pegga sounds huffy, like she's still mad at me. I guess she's holding a grudge about the way I treated her. Blaming her and then hanging up.

"Don't even mention Diana to me," I say to her in a low voice, in case my mom's eavesdropping. "She made such a fuss over me—and my mom too—like I might *die* or something. But I think my hand's getting better."

Pegga's being very quiet.

"It's too bad you weren't at the clinic today," I say to her. "We could have played Pretty-Ugly."

That's a game where Pegga and I flip through magazines looking at all the glossy ads, and decide who's geeky-looking and who's kind of cute. We have to say why and we have to pick a favorite at the end, of all the "pretties" and all the "uglies." There's a "boy" category and a "girl" one. The game is what made me like Pegga in the first place, because she always picked real-looking people, not the stick-thin ones with too much makeup or fake smiles.

"Sorry," she says. "Maybe the next time Odin bites you." And there's a click.

She's joking, right? I *meant* to apologize. She just didn't give me a chance.

9
It's All about the Hat

Saturday morning I'm up brrrr-ight and early. The brrrr part is that it's cold out, with fog everywhere. I can see my breath puff-puffing in front of my face.

Odin's grumbling along beside me with his blanket on. He'd rather be doing what Sonja is—sleeping in. So would I.

But to *not show up* at the Pet Safe sale is not even a consideration. I would rather die than admit to Sam that Odin and I have lately been in a heap of trouble. *Sorry, Sam, I couldn't make it because a) Odin was writhing in pain after an Elvis-attack. Or b) Then I was bitten by Odin in a super-bad mood. Or c) We were both grounded for our bad manners, bad attitude, whatever* . . . Right. Like any of that is ever going to come out of my mouth and disappoint Sam on the subject of Odin. No way.

Lucky for me, my mom's working. And my dad was so absent-minded this morning, I doubt he'll remember exact details. He had a couple of pals from work coming over to talk shop, as he said. He was in the best mood, cracking eggs and frying enough bacon for an army.

He said that if I behaved myself, he didn't think I'd be grounded for the whole weekend. But I should check with Mom first.

"Sure thing, Dad," I said, grabbing a few muffins in passing through the kitchen.

I figure he more or less gave me permission to leave the house. That's the story I'm sticking to, anyway. Just in case I get caught, I'll pretend it was a misunderstanding.

First stop on my way to the mall is the laundromat. I want to fancy Odin up a bit from the mudball he is. My mom said "that dirty old thing"—his new blanket, already filthy—wasn't going into *her* washer and dryer.

I watch all the mud spin around in the soapy water. Next, the blanket goes into an extractor, which spins most of the water out before I toss it into the dryer, so it won't shrink to piglet size.

Odin's getting antsy sitting by the door, and keeps smacking his lips impatiently. He has to shove over whenever someone goes in or out. It's amazing how many people wash their sweat suits and towels and baby sleepers early on a Saturday.

"You know, a pig shouldn't really be in here," says a gravelly voice.

I look at this guy with long greasy hair and a whole swarm of tattoos on his arms. I can't exactly tie Odin to a lamp-post out on the sidewalk. First squeal of brakes or loud, thumping rapper music from a passing car, and he'd freak out.

"He's not just a dumb pet," I say snarkily. "In fact, pigs are smarter than . . . some humans." Right away, I wish I hadn't.

The guy's eyes are jumping around in his head like he's swallowed a sparkler. Maybe he drinks too much coffee or doesn't sleep enough.

"Hey, look who's talking," he says. "Miss Smarty-pants herself."

I stand closer to a woman with a frizzy perm who's folding mountains of clothes. I wish Odin's blanket would hurry up. I can hear it going kerplunk, kerplunk, as it flops around in the dryer.

I decide to ignore Mr. Tattoo and try to look busy reading the bulletin board. There are notices for apartments to rent, and guitar lessons, and used cars for sale. One ad catches my eye: it's a smudgy photograph of an old delivery truck. And on its side is painted a red pig, a flying one, with small red flapping wings. The ad is weeks old and all the little paper tabs for phone numbers have been ripped off. Someone's probably bought it as a fixer-upper project; my dad used to do that. He'd spiffy some old classic car up, just for fun, and then sell it to someone who liked to drive antique cars in parades and stuff.

I find a poster Pet Safe has hung up: **Too Many Exotic Pets Dying of Starvation!**

Sam told me it's not always a case of not enough food—sometimes it's the wrong kind. People just don't know better. They'll feed tinned cat food when an animal needs live dragonflies or white mice, that sort of thing. Snakes and lizards look so thin anyway, I guess nobody notices until they're suddenly belly up.

I look down at Odin, pass him half of my bran muffin. I figure that's got to be good for him.

Odin's making a big mess of crumbs by the door until even Perm Lady gives us a dirty look. I figure it's time to go. The blanket's mostly dry anyway, and Odin snuggles into it with happy noises: *arree-arree-arree*. Mr. Tattoo blows us a kiss as we go out the door. Weird.

When we arrive at the mall it's still early—not many parked cars yet. Pet Safe has set up a couple of tables with things like old lamps and cameras, mismatched china cups and saucers, lace doilies, and Readers' Digest books that nobody wants to read. There's a rack of clothes too—all too bright and the wrong styles, as if they were never in fashion.

I can tell who Mrs. Bing is right away: she's the one unpacking things in a flurry from boxes and sticking prices on everything. She has smooth black hair like a helmet. It makes her look all business.

She's giving instructions to a thin, stooped fellow

who looks like a leftover from the peace-love generation with his tie-dyed jeans. So he must be helping too.

I feel stupid just standing there, so I flip through a few old Batman comics.

"Real collectors' items," a man with a shaggy gray beard tells me. He gives Odin the once-over, chuckles and says, "Would he like a pork-pie hat?"

I'm about to protest; Odin will hate someone fussing over him. But the fellow gets down on one knee and says hi to Odin like a real gentleman. Then he puts a wide-brimmed straw hat at an angle on Odin's head. It ties under the chin with a colorful scarf.

Whatever kind of hat it is, pork-pie or not, Odin actually seems to like it. He snarfs away contentedly, and makes funny faces, as if he's trying it on for size. Maybe the wide brim keeps him from seeing scary shadows coming up behind, sort of like horse blinkers.

I say thanks, and an older woman with a strange hat herself—green felt, with a small feather in the band—takes a picture of Odin. He cocks his head, as though he's posing.

"What's his name?" she asks.

"Odin," I say.

"Oh, that's interesting . . ." she says. "Odin's a famous character in folk tales . . . in Norway and parts of Europe. I remember stories when I was growing up—the name means *Wish*."

"Wow—I thought Odin was just a hokey farm-pig name," I admit.

Then Mrs. Bing comes over and hands me a metal cookie tin with a picture of Lassie on the lid. Inside are bills clipped into groups of twenties, tens, and fives. A mass of coins jangle all over the bottom.

"Tammy, so glad you could make it. I'd visit with your friend here—" she gives Odin an approving smile, "but I'm in a total flap right now. Can you make change?"

"I think so," I mutter. Math isn't exactly my biggest skill.

"Most things have prices," she says. "But people will bargain—just use your common sense. Don't give things away—but a dollar here or there doesn't matter."

And she leaves me with the money tin and a stack of paper bags, and some recycled plastic ones, all scrunched up.

"I'm going to be taking memberships—call me if you need help," Mrs. Bing adds, over her shoulder.

The first crowd of early-bird shoppers pokes through the old paperbacks and clunky jewelry on the table. Nearby I can see people trying on ski boots and making a fuss over an old hand saw. Some of the geekiest things are flying off the tacky clothes rack.

A young couple try on cowboy hats; it must be hat day or something. They're talking in western movie slang. "Yep, that's right, Slim. You betcha . . ."

The hats make them look goofy, but they end up buying them anyway, because it's for a good cause. They look like they're kind of in love. Like Sam and Sonja used to be.

A whole bunch of kids younger than me starts crowding around Odin. He doesn't seem to mind because they're short and smell like candy. They're asking me all sorts of questions. *What does he eat? Does he like cats and dogs? Where does he sleep? Can pigs get colds? What does he weigh?*

"What does Odin weigh? Well, it's hard to say. Right now, he's a little over 110 pounds, give or take—I have to weigh him by putting his front feet on the bathroom scales, and then his back end, and adding the numbers up—"

Odin's small audience is grinning—and growing. He's drawing people like a magnet. Not only animal-lovers, but even people just drifting by, getting distracted by all the commotion around a pot-bellied pig.

I tell them about water hyacinths and Odin's black cat friend, and Elvis the grouch, and the way Odin messes up his bed. I explain that the male pot-belly is smaller than the female. And how Vietnamese people prefer smaller, finer-boned pigs to the big, pinkish English ones. The European pigs would suffer too much from the heat in Vietnam, I say.

It's like I'm doing a practice run of my speech, except in little bits and pieces, and everyone is giving me an A. I'm blushing all over the place, I'm so pleased.

"Wow, you've really done your homework," the hippy fellow says. "And he's sure hamming it up," he adds, pointing at Odin. He introduces himself as Frank, and shakes my hand firmly, which makes me wince a little. Good thing it's on the mend.

Frank says he has a cockatiel at home that he rescued from a nasty pet shop. He figures he and the bird were supposed to meet up. That it was fate.

"I feel that way about Odin too," I say. And I realize I do.

Odin's grunting away, pleased with all the attention—maybe too pleased. I have to watch what people are trying to feed him: bits of hot dog—*Hold the mustard*—and peanuts, jujubes, spicy pepperoni sticks—*No, that'll make him sick. No Mars Bars, either—no, chocolate's not good for them*—

I don't even notice the time passing. People buy raffle tickets, they put handfuls of quarters and dimes, even five-dollar bills, into the basket with the Save-the-Tiger fridge magnets.

The big sale of the day is an old set of dining chairs, with seats so worn-out you can see the springs sticking up.

"Oh, sure, they need recovering, but they're a great deal," a woman says, standing back and eyeing the scruffy chairs as if they're great works of art. They sell for twenty-five dollars each, and Mrs. Bing makes a you-never-know face at me.

"This is our best Saturday ever," Frank swears when we're packing up. "Pet Safe made a killing."

"Yes, sirree," Mrs. Bing agrees. "Either it was the good weather, once that fog cleared, or it was—"

They both take a long hard look at Odin.

"You and Odin were quite a sensation," Mrs. Bing says to me. "You wouldn't consider coming by again, would you? Bringing along your friend?"

She's rolling coins and putting elastics around the bills.

"Here's something for your time," she says. "A little commission for Odin. Sam tells me you take such good care of him. And he must cost you a few pennies—"

She hands me a ten-dollar bill. I make a face as if I want to protest. But the money stays neatly folded in my hand. After all, I spent tons of quarters cleaning Odin's blanket. And I owe Pegga.

"We normally have a sale once a month," Mrs. Bing says. "But there's a special seminar on cold-weather care of tropical animals. And soon we have our Christmas craft and bake sales coming up. So we're in business every other Saturday for the next while. Would you be interested?"

"Sure thing," I say, as though I have all the time in the world, and the best marks at school. As though I am *not* grounded, as though I am *bound to own Odin the pig forever*. It feels good to believe all of that.

I suddenly realize by the time on Mrs. Bing's watch how late it is. Well past noon already.

"But right now I have to run—you know, help my mom with dinner."

I don't even know why I say that last bit. But lately I've been feeling as though I have to convince people that I'm doing something right. And then it seems something always goes wrong, and I have to keep convincing them. I always want to add to the truth.

In my rush to get home, I forget all about returning Odin's straw hat. He wears it at a slant all the way back to our house.

Odin does *not* become a ham on a platter at Thanksgiving, as Sonja once predicted. And by some sort of freaky luck, no one mentions the Pet Safe sale, either.

I spend the rest of Saturday cleaning out my dad's van, making oodles of orange-smelling bubbles with this fancy carpet cleaner goop. Odin practically gets woozy on the stuff, and dances a little jig, chasing the bubbles. And my dad and I get into a water fight, throwing soapy sponges back and forth.

I guess he had a great visit with his friends from

work; they were celebrating the good news. With a few more weeks of physio, the doctor told him, he'll be able to supervise down at the mill again, at least part-time. My dad's almost giddy with relief.

"I'm on a roll!" he says, hitting me square on the chin with a sopping sponge.

"I'm on a roll too!" I sputter through the suds, heaving the sponge back, a trail of bubbles arcing through the air.

And to prove it, I even start to clean up my room after I've finished the van. I tidy up the piles of clothes, dishes, stacks of CDs, and mismatched shoes, dirty socks. Even the piggy ones from Pegga.

Oh, yeah, Pegga. I really should call her and make up.

I practice a couple of times so I can get my apology in before she fades out on me again. When someone picks up at the other end, I sound like some sort of sprinter on the phone. "Pegga-listen-I'm-so-sorry-I-thought-you-told-my mother!"

It's *her* mother. Oops.

"Tammy, I'll just get Pegga," she says, as though I'm acting totally normal.

"Hello?" Pegga says, in a friendly voice.

I plunge in again.

"Pegga, listen, I'm so-so-so-so sorry that I thought . . ."

"I know," she cuts in. "It's okay. I can see why you were bugged. I was kind of showing off, with Walter and his brother's friends, the whole freaky film crew . . . Do you want to come over?"

"I can't—I'm grounded. At least I think I am. So I'm cleaning up my room."

"Are you *feeling* all right?" Pegga asks.

We laugh, and it's right back to where we should be. Friends again.

"No problem, " she adds. "I'll come over and help."

And she does. She helps me organize everything, so I can open my closet door without things falling out. She stores things I'm not using, like my summer clothes, in plastic containers under my bed. It's like a room makeover.

We even use a little more of the bubbly stuff on my own dingy carpet. By the time we're finished, the whole house smells like an orange grove.

My mom's so pleased when she looks in the door, she looks like the pretty photograph in her bedroom when she's ten years younger. In fact, she's still pleased with me by the time Thanksgiving dinner gets put on the table the next night. Along with sizzling turkey, there's fresh-pressed cranberry sauce the special way my mom makes it, with orange rind. So, it's more oranges in the air.

My mother even winks at me once, when she asks me to pass the brussels sprouts.

"You can save yours for You-know-who," she adds. She knows why I've been rolling mine around on the plate. First off, because I hate them, and secondly, because Odin loves them to pieces.

Even Sonja's being nice to me, as if she's intent on setting some sort of sweet-sister record. We spend the whole weekend overeating and then counting calories. She's doing some sort of nutrition project for school. We lose track at about 10,000 calories between the two of us.

"We're supposed to eat two thousand a day, tops," Sonja says. "Even if we're so-called growing, or doing sports. And just one piece of pumpkin pie heaped with whipped cream is probably half that . . . Oops."

Monday, my mom's back at work, but Pegga comes over for "catch-as-catch-can"—my mother's name for leftovers. The dinner my dad puts together is almost as big as the feast we had on Thanksgiving. Turkey and gravy, and baked yams galore, Odin bound to get all the skins.

Pegga almost blows it when she puts on Odin's tie-under-the-chin straw hat and says "thank you" in Korean: *kamsa-hamnida.*

I don't blame her. I nearly forget, myself, that the Pet Safe sale—where Odin got his hat—is still a secret.

"Speaking of other languages," I say, careful not to trip myself up, "someone told me some neat stuff the other day about Odin's name."

"Oh, didn't you know what his name meant?" Sonja asks.

She leaps into the conversation as if Odin's her

favorite topic: "He's a god-like creature who puts spells on trolls and giants; those were the bad guys in the old Norse legends."

"And listen to this," Sonja says, whispering softly, so that Pegga and I lean closer. "There's a story where one of his eyes gets gouged out or something, I forget exactly—just so he can keep a promise he made. He's really big on that—being true to your word."

"No pain, no gain," my dad says, pitching in.

I poke him in the ribs. Meanwhile Pegga's cupping a hand over one eye, taking a one-eyed look at the bunch of us round the table.

"You should ask Sam more about the story," Sonja adds, as if it doesn't even hurt her to say so. "That's who told me—when he first rescued Odin last summer." She looks almost happy to be mentioning his name. Maybe it's all the turkey and stuffing or something.

10

Pot-bellies Make the World Go Round

I'm feeling almost confident about giving my little talk, as Diana calls our speeches. At least until lunchtime, when Walter Cluster insists I'm going to be *mind-boggling* on the subject of pigs.

I have a sudden urge to run through my presentation one last time. To remind myself of all the details in the right order. I figure that's hard to do at school, with everyone yacking away. So I pack up my sandwich—tuna salad with too many pickles—and sprint home.

My dad's nowhere to be seen. He's probably at his physio class or running errands. He's been cooped up so long that driving anywhere, even to buy milk or drop off videos, seems exciting.

I guess my dad forgot to feed Odin his lunch, because he's making all these harrumphing noises; it's amazing how grumpy he gets when he's hungry. He's shoulder-checking the garage door, knows exactly where his food tin is, high up on a shelf above the workbench, out of reach. Otherwise he'd just help himself.

I go over my speech while Odin's slurping his pellets down with the slushy backwash in his water bowl. I'm feeling pretty sure of my facts. I know that pot-bellies have their sway-backed shape to hold all the swampy roughage they eat—the stalks of water hyacinth, lentils, potatoes, and a ton of other root vegetables, some I'd never heard of before—like *manioc* and *taro*. The pigs' tummies sometimes sweep the ground, so Odin shouldn't feel bad about his bow-legged way of walking.

Then I start to feel cluttered with information, as if I might know *too much* now about pot-bellies. The more I look over my notes, the more I get all mixed up. What exactly *are* mangrove swamps? Do pigs eat ginger root or do people eat pork roast with ginger?

I'm going to sound stupid spitting out words like "sow" or "boar." Kids are going to be sniggering, with Diana tsk-tsking away in the background. Why did I even dream of tackling this subject? Out loud, in front of everyone? I suddenly have a bad case of nerves.

Who am I kidding? I *have* to do this. So I can get a

fantastic mark, and every time the subject of Odin comes up, my mother thinks: Tammy + Odin = Good Student! like some sort of happy equation.

My mouth goes dry. I start to clear my throat over and over, as though I might be losing my voice.

And then it hits me. What could be better than a hands-on presentation, a sort of pig show-and-tell? Sheer inspiration! I mean, you can describe going to Mars all you want, but until you actually put on a spacesuit and ship out in a rocket, you probably don't really get it.

Odin's already snoozing in his dried-out puddle by the back steps in a blissful moment of autumn sun. He can be eating one minute and keel over the next. He's the master of the short-and-deep sleep.

I give him a tickle under the chin, ask him for a big favor.

"Come on, Odin. It'll be a gas. Probably some yummy lunch leftovers."

I take the dried mud off his face, tidy him up a bit with one of my mom's tea towels. I struggle to put on his harness, pulling one unwilling foreleg, then the other.

I take a quick look in the composting pail: only a few apple peelings. So I grab a half-cluster of grapes from the fridge. I'm going to need to bribe Odin. He's not in a big mood for an outing, I can tell.

He can feel that I'm in a rush too, with no time to

dawdle. I'm pulling him along, with a fake-cheerful voice: "Come on, Odie. That's a fella. Hurry, come on."

We cut through a few back lanes, where Odin wants to sniff every garbage can and check out each shadow. Already he's making his worried noise, saying his little high-pitched mantra while we scuttle across the ball field and then zig-zag through the parking lot of good old Lowther Middle School.

Odin sees himself reflected in the glass doors of the side entrance by the gym. I guess he doesn't like what he sees, because he harffs out his red-alert sound. I manage to pull him inside the doors. He doesn't want to budge. The floors have just been waxed to ice-rink perfection and his little split feet, sounding like teeny tiny high heels, are slipping and sliding all over the place.

A couple of grade nines wearing ditzy halter tops make these freaked-out faces. They clutch each other and shriek, "What's that?" It's like they've never seen a pig before.

Odin finds it all too much. The smell of the Tex-Mex food the cooking class has served up, the racket of lockers slamming, the end-of-lunch buzzer droning on and off, like a giant mosquito.

By now Odin's full-out squealing. He starts whirling around in circles, gets his legs all tangled up in the leash trying to make quick dashes at the glass doors. He's making such a fuss thrashing about, it looks as though I'm torturing him, as though I don't know the first thing about pigs.

The worst thing is Mr. Bentwhistle, the Vice, coming along in a big hurry. He's tall—basketball-player tall. And he has a booming voice that seems to echo when he speaks. His open suit jacket is flying behind him as if he's skiing down the hallway.

"Young lady, you must be aware there are rules that forbid—*a pig* coming into the school!" he shouts out. He's overreacting like crazy, as though I've come to school naked or I'm waving a knife in my hand.

I mutter something about Odin being at the heart of a very important project. "Everyone in room 210 is waiting—" I say, still flustered by Odin's frantic display.

Mr. B. is "outraged," as he says. No kidding. "I want you to take that—*animal*—outside right now! I shouldn't have to repeat myself, young lady—"

He doesn't have to repeat it. I'm being jostled by Odin in his pig panic. He's gotten one of his pointy trotters caught in the rubber boot-scraper, and we go flapping out the door.

I mutter over my shoulder, "If I get a failing mark—well, it won't be *my* fault."

I don't know whose fault it'll be *but* mine. Still, I'm feeling totally sorry for myself. It seemed like such a good idea.

And now there's only my very noticeable absence in Miss Pickles' class, with everyone guessing where I might be—whether I'm dying of stage fright or have just plain forgotten. I'm hooped. Even if I run home like a maniac, I doubt I can get back fast enough to give my speech.

Odin's slobbering all down his front, like he does when he's scared. And suddenly I'm ashamed that I dragged him through this shabby performance. I mean, the whole shouting match with Mr. Bentwhistle, the slippery floors, how I tried to rush Odin into an unfamiliar place. That's the first thing it says in my pot-bellies book: "Convince your pig with gentle persuasion, get down on your knees and use a coaxing tone of voice, or food tidbits. Never, never try to force your pig!"

I should know all that. How sensitive Odin is. How could I have forgotten? That was the whole point of the project, wasn't it? To understand pot-bellies, and teach people—especially my mother—that I know all about caring for one.

Right there on the spot, I give myself a C grade for insight. I get down on one knee and say to Odin, "Sorry, buddy."

But he's still worried, and I've run out of grapes to calm him down. So I let myself be dragged down the sidewalk. Odin squints at me over one shoulder, his tail twitching with indignation.

Just then Walter Cluster sticks his head out of the classroom window above me and hollers, "Hang on! Hang on!—Wow, what a great idea!"

I haven't the faintest clue what he's talking about, but I pull Odin to a stop. Odin's snorting impatiently. He wants to get home—now.

Then I see the most amazing thing. Out the side door of the school comes my whole class in a quiet line, like some sort of slowed-down fire drill, with Miss Pickles leading the way. They head to the space on the lawn where we sometimes eat our lunches. The whole class sits, with Walter Cluster beaming at me like this is the neatest thing ever.

"What a nice surprise—" Miss Pickles says. "But you really should have warned us, Tammy. If Walter hadn't said that your project was outside, waiting . . ."

"I couldn't get him up the stairs," I mumble. I don't mention my run-in with Mr. Bentwhistle, and having broken some sort of rule about pigs at school.

Odin's still scowling, holding a grudge. There are too many people gawking at him and no food treats, so he's decided to stick his nose up in the air with disapproval. Everyone laughs except Missy Miles, who's sitting cross-legged in the front row, cringing while Odin makes his grumpy faces.

I just launch into my speech, to get it over with. And I have to say that the four minutes fly by as if I'm on automatic pilot. I don't even remember what I say. Something about pot-bellies having a sharper sense of smell than the pinky kind of farm pigs. And that the old wild pigs—the kind you read about in fairy tales—were more active, could run up to 25 miles an hour in short dashes.

"Though I'm not sure how anyone would have known—long before there were cars or stopwatches—exactly how fast a pig was running," I add.

"Good point," Walter Cluster says.

"Hush up, Walter Cluster, we want to hear," says a chorus of voices.

And it's true, they *do* want to hear. The class seems to listen to every word. And at the end I get applause—not just polite clapping—but real enthusiasm. I'm relieved, but it makes Odin jumpy all over again. Especially as everyone crowds around him afterward, wanting to pat him and feel his bristly skin.

"One or two at a time, " I warn. "Otherwise he gets scared."

I show people how to tickle him under the chin, how to give him a tummy scratch. The best part is when Miss Pickles looks deep into Odin's squinty eyes and says, "He appears to have a sweet disposition, he really does."

Then she seems to remember where she is, with a bunch of grade eights and a pig, out on the lawn. Cars in front of the school are slowing down to see what's up.

"Well, class, that's it," she says, patting her wind-blown bun back into place. "This isn't a picnic or a whole afternoon's excursion—but an exception we made, so that Tammy could tell us about Odin. And I have to say, it was very educational to see him—in the flesh."

"Good pun," Walter blurts out.

"Hush, Walter Cluster," the same chorus pipes up.

Miss Pickles continues, "Now Tammy, you have to hurry Odin home and run back lickety-split, so you're not late for your next class. And the rest of us are returning to the classroom for the next presentation—Missy? Are you ready?"

Missy doesn't look too ready for anything. She's

still frozen on the grass, her nose crinkled up at the sight of Odin.

"She looks like she's stuck in her own personal lotus position," Pegga whispers to me. I roll my eyes back at her.

Odin's anxious to get going. He breaks into a clip-clopping trot, pulling me down the street, proving that theory about pigs being fast when push comes to shove. It's only when he seems to be limping a little that he slows down. He's panting lightly as we turn the corner. I'm worried—pigs overheat so easily. You'd think he'd know that. But I guess with all the excitement he's had, he's just like a little kid—wants to get home, where it's safe and cozy, for a nap.

We're waiting for the light to change and I crouch beside Odin on the sidewalk, give him a little pep talk. "Hey, chin up, buddy. The main thing is—we both survived. And I'll make it up to you with lots of treats!"

And that's when it happens, when we're only a block from home.

I remember the white truck with a picture of a pig on its side—a chubby flying pig, a red one—zooming by.

"Hey, that's the same truck as the ad in the laundromat," I say aloud. As if Odin cares a hoot, or is bound to agree.

I remember thinking how strange, what a coincidence. As if the truck is a sign or something. I'll never forget that part. And then the truck with the flying pig backfires, really loudly. Like a gunshot.

Odin practically jumps out of his skin, as if he's being shot from a cannon. *And somehow I lose my grip on the leash.* And Odin's suddenly running—full speed, with his leash trailing—*across the street, in front of oncoming traffic.* Even though it's actually happening, it seems like a bad dream, as if I can't move, can't wake up.

My face freezes in horror as I watch Odin scuttle between cars veering around him. A downtown bus lurches to an abrupt stop. But he actually makes it to the other side of the street, his short, squat body squeezing between a couple of parked cars. It's a miracle.

Before the light even changes, I run like an Olympic sprinter across the crosswalk. The bus pulls away, the driver shaking his head. I guess it's not every day he narrowly misses hitting a pig on the loose. And sees a deranged kid running after it.

"Odie!" I shout out. "Here, boy—come on, it's all right."

I look up the sidewalk one way, and then down the street in the other direction. There's no Odin in sight.

Aha, I think! The vacant lot, with its mess of weeds and mounds of dirt—that's where Odin's scurried off to. And he's hiding. Keeping a low profile.

But after chasing around, poking through clumps of nettles and blackberries, and calling out Odin's name a kazillion times in as cheerful a tone as I can—so he doesn't think I'm mad at him for running away—there's still no sign of him. I even check out the hedges and gardens bordering the seniors' home. Not a grunt, not a rustle of garbage, no hint of Odin.

Impossible, I think. And then I remember the part in my speech about how fast pigs can run. Almost race-horse fast.

I sit down in a sandpile and cry my eyes out. Which may sound like I give up. But I don't.

I run all the way home, sweating like crazy, my heart pounding. But I don't really believe he'll be there. And he isn't.

So I sit on the back steps, right by Odin's patch of sunlight. Where he would be sleeping if I hadn't messed things up. And I think over and over, because I don't know what else to do—*this can't be happening.*

It's the one thing I never imagined, when I imagined losing Odin. That I would actually *lose* Odin.

11
Missing

My mom's face gets squeezed into this pretend grin when she sees me. She whispers into the phone, "Thank you, Miss Pickles." Then she starts humming and wiping off the kitchen counter, trying to look casual.

I guess this is my mom's way of keeping a secret. She doesn't want to upset me, but I already know what the fuss is about. Diana and my mother are concerned about my attendance—I've been skipping classes, and not exactly enjoying myself even when I do show up.

I can't seem to pay attention at school. I'm sure my marks are going down, down, down. But getting good grades doesn't matter anymore. Even the fact that I got an A from Miss Pickles for my speech about pot-bellies is pointless somehow. I feel tired all the time, exhausted, as though I'm running a race and someone keeps moving the finish line. I keep forgetting assignments or falling asleep. And when I drift off—last time it was in science class, with my head on my desk—I wake up jumpy and nervous. And I'm always thinking the same thing.

Where *is* Odin?

That's the prickly question of every hour in every day. Nothing else matters. Other pieces of information or conversation, unrelated to Odin, just bounce off my ears. I say, *yes, please,* or *no, thank you* to questions of *Ketchup? Green beans? Ride to school?* I see people's mouths moving, but the voices sound underwater, words washing in and out like some sort of ocean background, like the faint swish, swish, swish in a giant seashell.

Pegga says someone's a dork, and I think she said "pork." The sound of my mother scraping carrots reminds me of the scratchy sound of Odin's tummy rubbing over the back stairs—and I race outside, run warm water into his bowl just the way he likes it, in case he shows up, thirsty as can be. I don't want him to think I've forgotten him.

My mother's worried. She watches me as though I'm shape-shifting in front of her, turning into a different girl. The other day she gasped when she saw my Odin shrine: the itsy-bitsy paper fortunes from Howard's fortune cookies, and a cluster of grapes, getting musty, along with my framed picture of jowly old Odin and a large bamboo ladle.

"It's supposed to be good luck in Korea," I told my

mom. "Pegga loaned it to me. It's been in her family a long time; it's a special kind you hang on the wall, just to keep your home safe."

And of course my shrine has a candle burning at all times. My mom started fussing, so I've enclosed what she called a "fire hazard" in an old hurricane lantern I found stashed in the basement.

"That's more ticky-boo," my mom said, whatever that means.

The candle flickers day and night.

"The little flame cheers me up," I told Pegga the other day. "It's something about hope."

She'd dropped by with a huge stack of homework. "Now *that's* a fire hazard," I said glumly.

She started waving around a black feather, tickling my nose with it, trying to make me laugh. I guess Pegga's worried about me too.

"In Asia, there's a special kind of magpie," she said, "and if you hear their song, you're supposed to get your wish." Then she started cackling and shrieking like a Pegga-bird, flapping her arms up and down, just to cheer me up.

When she finished squawking, she placed the black feather in the Odin shrine. "It's a crow's, but whatever," she said.

I didn't mind her goofing around. Odin needs all the luck he can get. Like the letter from Sam. It's in my Odin shrine too.

I've never gotten a letter in the mail before, other than Christmas cards from my aunt or a postcard I got once from Pegga that said, "Aloha from Hawaii!" I don't count the formal notice I got from Mr. Bentwhistle explaining the rule about pigs. It's because of hygiene, he said, and people having allergies, and animals being unpredictable. Just so I'd know the next time.

Now there *is* no next time.

At one point, I'd have been thrilled to get any kind of personal note from Sam. But now the subject's so gloomy, it almost spoils the fact that he put goofy doodles of stick girls and not-so-stickish pigs on the envelope just to make me smile.

Hi Tammy:
Listen, don't blame yourself, okay? I know you've taken really good care of Odin. And that you'll find him—safe and sound. Promise me you won't get too down about this. It'll all turn out fine. Just keep thinking about the good karma thing. As if Odin's protected in a kind of bubble, okay? I'm keeping my fingers crossed.
Hugs, Sam

Sam's note and Odin's fat-cheeked picture were supposed to go into my disaster kit at school. But I've decided to keep half of my Tammy-kit at home, and told Miss Pickles so—I mean, that's where disaster struck.

And comfort is why I'm sleeping with Odin's blanket; it lies on my bed like some sort of piggy quilt. Sometimes I imagine him under it, snoring away. But my mother's not keen on this new habit of mine, either.

"It's clean," I told her. "Well—sort of. It got washed not long before he was—*stolen*."

She started to say something, but then changed her mind. She's been trying her best to be supportive. She's always offering me mugs of soup or baking cookies for me, right out of the blue. Hermits, my favorites. But they seem like tasteless lumps now, no matter how many chocolate chips or raisins she plops into the batter.

Hermits seem boring, and Odin seems *stolen.* That's how I think of it; that Odin's been *taken* from me.

My head hurts like crazy, like an on-and-on headache, whenever I sort through what might or might not have happened the day Odin disappeared. Sometimes I can't stand all the confusion. First I think I remember Odin being snatched at the bus stop, even the bus driver somehow in cahoots with the thief, blocking my view, and then thundering off with a puff of exhaust, Odin vamoosed. Then I think I recall a fire truck rushing by, the sirens driving Odin farther and farther down the street, until I can no longer see him. I faintly remember a huge gust of wind and a dust storm, like the kind they have on the Sahara, where you can't breathe and a whole car is covered by sand in a second, and by the time the dust settles, no Odin. In another flashback, it's like an old fairy tale, Elvis chasing Odin, Elvis the size of a dragon, a blast of flames rushing out of his mouth. Which only leads me to think of the fire trucks again. I keep going round and round in circles. I think of Mr. Tattoo at the laundromat, who clearly didn't like Odin. I think of Odin's fan club at the Pet Safe sale, all those people who *did* like him.

The only answer to Odin's mysterious disappearance is that he's been *stolen.* I mean, even if someone found him, he's not theirs to keep—so he's been snatched by someone, plain and simple. Someone has Odin who *shouldn't* have Odin.

That's what I keep telling my mom and dad, and Pegga and Walter . . . even Sonja believes me, I can tell—that someone must have grabbed Odin, right out of our yard. Maybe at gunpoint or tied up with duct tape in a burlap sack, squealing the whole way. That's what I keep thinking, that Odin came home and someone kidnapped him, is maybe holding him for ransom. That it's a cheap trick or weird prank, and we just haven't received the threatening note in the mail yet, or the freaky phone call with a muffled voice.

I can't even bear to think about it sometimes when I retrace my steps—how I take Odin to school, the presentation on the lawn at Lowther with Odin champing at the bit to get home, how I bend down to pat him at the corner just a block from my house, how the truck backfiring makes him stampede across the street and I'm right behind him . . . and home is clearly where he's heading . . . and then poof, *no Odin!*

The story keeps shifting and resettling, shifting and resettling.

But I know this much. I know it's not my fault. It can't be. I simply can't accept that *I did this to Odin.* No way.

Odin's brief moments of fame—at the Pet Safe sale, and then showing up for my class project—have only succeeded in making him a well-known tragic figure. On the very day Odin disappears, his picture ends up on the front page of the local paper as the Pet Safe mascot.

It bugs me at first that Mrs. Bing didn't even ask my permission. But the picture has come in handy—in the Lost and Found section. His jowly face is now an ad for: **MISSING PIG!** Mascot for Pet Safe last seen *not wearing* his hat, MISSING from 1411 Plumtree Place. REWARD!!!!!

I've put up posters too, at the mall, at the library, in Howard Wong's front window—he said he was glad to help—and on every lamp-post and mailbox between here and Texas. I thought it might all have been a waste of time when I suddenly remembered the black cat. All at once I had a hunch that Odin might have scooted into the wrong yard, just three houses down from ours.

Mrs. Dalton, the ancient lady who owns the cat, probably thinks I'm weird now for always staring at her porch, and even crawling underneath it once, whispering, "Odin, are you there?" Of course there was no pig there—just a lot of spiders—even though I kept crossing my fingers and asking Mrs. Dalton four hundred times a day whether she'd seen my pig. Any pig.

In fact, it's amazing how many people *have* seen a pig. There have been so many pig sightings I've had to organize all the information in a binder, as if Odin is a new subject at school, like math or history. So far, it's thirty-three reports of *maybe* seeing Odin, and still counting. I mark them in different colors of highlighter as to "still being possible" or "turned out to be a really fat dog," that sort of thing. I have columns for date and place, if people can remember, which they never can. They say, maybe last Tuesday, maybe three weeks ago. One person saw a "black pig with white spots at a farm in Langley—a few *years* ago," which doesn't really help.

It's a full-time job just sitting by the phone. Every day I phone the SPCA, and the dog pound, and every vet in town—Hill 'n' Dale, Pets Plus, Avonlea, Fraser Heights. They're so sick of hearing my voice, I've tried to disguise it. Sometimes I talk with a little-kid lisp, or with a bad French accent. One day a frosty voice reminded me that they would phone if Odin showed up, I could be *sure* of that. So I've had Pegga phone a few times, and Walter Cluster offered once. He said he had an interesting chat with a woman about an escaped iguana and forgot to ask about Odin—he's such a geek.

Every day I walk to every place that Odin's ever been, even the rec center where Pegga's mom teaches yoga classes. It made me cry buckets to remember how Pegga and I tried to teach Odin a pose: what we called Downward Facing Pig. We had a laughing fit at the way Odin did a small, hopeless bow to get the carrot we were offering him.

Every time I do my tour of the neighborhood—the mall where he might remember the oodles of treats at the Pet Safe sale, or the vacant lot behind Pleasantview, the nursing home—I think I'm there at the wrong time, that I've just missed seeing him. I even dropped in one day at Pleasantview. They were having a sing-along around a piano, and I was rude enough to ask whether anyone had seen a pig. One woman with bluish-gray hair *thought* she remembered seeing a *very big, very pink* pig. She said it was *oinking* loudly.

"Wrong pig," I had to tell her. "Odin doesn't really oink. And he's more of a mouse-gray color. Except way, way bigger than a mouse."

A couple of the grannies and grandpas just looked confused and started singing off-key again. What was I thinking? Maybe imaginary animals brighten up their days.

I just want to know what's happened to Odin—that he's not hurt or starving, or in some horrible greased pig contest. The other day I saw a TV ad for a fall fair down in Washington State, and they showed these idiot kids throwing themselves onto the bodies of terrified pigs slathered in oil. I broke out in itchy hives just thinking about Odin squealing his head off in that sort of situation.

My mother asked, "Tammy, is it something you ate? Are you coming down with something, a fever, some sort of rash?"

Then she offered me chicken soup and hermit cookies.

Oh, I was coming down with something all right. That's the night I had the terrible dream.

It's like the craziest supermarket in the whole world—masses of white chickens squawking and flapping in bamboo cages, huge piles of brightly colored fruit and thick carpets, with everyone in a hurry, dashing about. Everyone wearing the Odin straw hat, tied under their chins, all the men and women, and all the children too. It's Odin-hats galore.

And all the people under the hats are shouting in a foreign language. At first I think I'm dreaming in Vietnamese, and how strange that is. And there, suddenly, behind the curtain of a dark, cluttered shop that smells like old gym socks, in a bigger version of a chicken cage, is Odin's face staring out at me accusingly. As if his number's up, and it's all my fault.

The worst part is when he opens his mouth and real words come out—well, almost real words. In a slow-motion, blubbery voice he says, "Ease-play elp-hay e-may."

I wake up in a total sweat. Then I realize the dream-Odin was speaking in a kind of code. It's a sort of backwards English that was a fad when my dad's dad went to school way back when, just to drive the teachers bonkers, I guess. My dad and I used to goof around in it, trying to trip each other up. I don't why it was called Pig Latin—but my dream-Odin sure has it down pat. Garbled, yes, but he's asking for help, big-time.

The nightmare makes me more nervous than ever. My heart's actually pounding right out of my chest when I wake up and remember the dream, in jiggly pieces, as though it's part of a bigger puzzle. I have to do *something.* I just don't know what it is.

12

What's Wrong
with this Pig-ture?

Pegga's been trying to put some sparkle back into
my life. She has this kooky idea that we'll dress up for
this week's Free Friday. What she calls the film
"pree-miere."

It's Walter Cluster's so-called Big Day. Instead of the
horror flick he was keen on making, Walter and a
bunch of kids in our English class got all excited about
some contest called "Keep Our World Green."

"I'm tickled pink to see that your speeches led to
another project of your own making," Miss Pickles said
when she first heard about it. Everyone sniggered, just
to think of Miss Pickles being tickled. But the word *pink*
reminded me of pigs in general and Odin in particular,
so I felt shivery and sad.

I guess the contest is to see which school can send

the best message about a sustainable world, which means we can still live here for a while, without all the water being used up and the weather going freaky. The competition is offering prizes: a hundred dollars to each of the finalists. The final five films get shown in some sort of enviro-festival, too, whatever that is.

It seems like everyone is talking about the environment these days, and nothing but. Green-schmeen. I couldn't care less anymore about the stupid earth. It can roll itself into a big ball of garbage and global warming, for all the difference it makes to me. The earth is one flat place, where the sun never shines, without Odin.

I don't know much about the movie. I didn't exactly take part in any aspect of making it: it was mostly an after-school project. And I've been busy. Preoccupied. Or as my mother says, "down in the glooms." So I didn't act or shove lights around or help edit, like the computer geeks who blended all the pictures together at the end. I guess they spent hours making every detail fit, even though the film is only eight minutes long.

Pegga's been hinting like mad that there's going to be some sort of surprise when Walter lets the film roll. That's what gets her thinking that I need a makeover from living in my sweats. Sure, I say, why not?

I let Pegga twist my kinky hair into something like a hairdo, with a big clip and a fake rhinestone holding it in some sort of pretzel shape. And she pushes me into one of my mom's old dresses, actually feeds my arms through the armholes and wiggles the skirt onto my hips.

"Not bad," she says, stepping back to take a look. "You need a pair of heels."

"Are you kidding? I don't even own a pair."

"Well, you can't wear sneakers with a skirt at a film pree-miere," she says.

"At a real *pree-miere*," I remind her, "limos drive up to a red carpet, and famous people step out, wearing swanky gowns and tuxedos. And there are a lot of photographers with flashing cameras, and movie stars eating caviar and drinking champagne—"

"Sit still," Pegga says, brushing powdery, purplish blush on my cheeks.

"Whereas, in our case, Walter Cluster will be his usual know-it-all self, and it's bound to be juice and cookies in the classroom. Whoopee—"

Pegga's still fussing over me, tying a beaded choker round my neck. It's one she made herself. It's a turquoisey color that makes my eyes seem greener.

"Not too tight, or I'll feel like I'm choking," I say. "So, is Walter-the-Film-Director wearing a bowtie?"

"I doubt it," Pegga says. But we both snicker at the thought.

It's not as easy as it looks, I have to admit, as I wobble down the halls of Lowther on my mom's T-strap heels.

I just slipped the stupid things on, and I feel like I'm going to fall on my face.

"Keep your hips forward," Pegga says, walking so softly it's like she's on a surface of bubble wrap.

I lean too hard on a turn in the hall and almost keel over. Sure enough, I snap a heel right off my mother's shoe. I hobble into the classroom with one shoe off and one shoe on. It's just as well; my feet were hurting already. Note to self: it's torture to wear high heels.

Pegga's shaking her head. She's probably wondering whether it was worthwhile to even bother dressing me up.

But limping or not, Miss Pickles looks thrilled to see me.

I haven't even settled into my seat before Walter Cluster starts his spiel about the movie. He's wearing one of his pinstriped shirts, his corduroys sagging on his lanky legs. No bowtie. I have a brief image of him years from now accepting some big fat prize at the Cannes Film Festival, still wearing the same outfit, and thanking his grade eight class for his start as a famous director.

"This movie, *What's Wrong with this Pig-ture?* might seem comical," Walter explains, "but in every scene there's a hidden message. If you look closely behind our very special animal actor, Odin, you'll see the world we live in with different eyes. Remember, in each scene, the pig's the clue."

Everyone's hyper and clapping, even before the film

starts rolling. As though Walter Cluster is suddenly the class hero. But I just sit there, stunned. What's he talking about? What's the movie got to do with Odin?

I'm about to find out.

Right off the bat there's a picture of me walking down the sidewalk, Odin waddling along beside me, snuffling everywhere, getting tangled up in his leash. And me making faces at the film crew, shooing them away.

I feel a hot surge of tears behind my eyes. That was so long ago, when the weather was still warm, Walter's ditzy brother driving down my street and Walter leaning out the back window, filming my every idiotic move.

A mix of emotions goes back and forth, like ping-pong balls, inside me. I'm sad to see Odin looking so happy—and I'm mad at Walter but pleased too, that he actually had the nerve to put this in his stupid movie. It's so wonderful to see Odin that I have a lump in my chest, a hot potato where my heart should be. I'm suddenly looking forward to seeing the film, and dreading that it will end in only minutes.

In other words, I'm a total mess. I have to clamp my eyes shut a little, press my hand up to the mascara already sticking to my cheeks.

It turns out the whole movie is made up of Odin moments, his nose turned up, disapproving, just like Walter said. You have to laugh, even though the problems—like traffic congestion, or smokestacks spewing clouds of pollution—aren't really funny. Maybe that's what *edgy* is, funny overtop of serious.

It's as if Odin's smarter and less of a so-called *pig* than the people who are making the world more noisy and crowded and dirty every day. The shots of Odin making his usual faces are so neatly spliced into other scenes, it looks totally natural. At one point Odin grimaces at a leaf blower making a racket, even though he's never met up with a leaf blower in real life. And Walter plops Odin's "happy face" into a park scene, with birds twittering and children playing, the clattering traffic noises fading into the background. There's even a nifty shot in Chinatown near the end.

The movie ends with a close-up of Odin's fat tummy swaying from side to side, practically brushing the sidewalk, and the words: Hokus Porkus Productions. Then the credits start to roll. They list everyone who held a light or pointed a camera or played a ten-second bit as a "sidewalk sweeper" or "urban gardener," the two roles Pegga played. And then I see my own name too, Tammy Rose Gifford, listed as both "the girl with the pig" and "animal trainer."

The lights come on in the room. I'm trying to hide my case of snuffles, and everyone else in the room is good enough not to stare at me. They're all *ecstatic*—that's Pegga's latest word—with the way the film turned out.

Miss Pickles has a wide smile that's sailing right off her face.

"I'm really impressed," she says. "It's thoughtful and quite amusing in parts . . . You should all be proud of your achievement."

Everyone's talking all at once, and Walter is gorging himself on Oreos, with a glazed look of happiness in his eyes. He's explaining, with too much cookie stuffed into his cheek, why he used Chinatown for the last section of the movie.

"I made a wide sweep with my camera," he says, "and got nothing but bicycles, and colorful markets, with people walking—not a single car in sight. So I thought, hey, this is good—and it's the one part in the movie where I didn't have to edit my Odin pics into place. I didn't have to—I mean, how freaky is that?" he muses. "That I should have found an Odin look-alike in Chinatown on the very day I was shooting—"

And then it hits me—

"Go back!" I scream.

Everyone in the room looks shocked and stares at me.

"Rewind the film . . . you're wrong! That's Odin! The pig in Chinatown—it is *so* Odin!"

Someone dims the lights again. Walter Cluster rewinds the film slowly back through the credits and to a scene that hazily drifts past a restaurant named The Golden Buddha, and then focuses in on a pig . . .

It's Odin, no doubt about it. I'd recognize his jowls anywhere—and that way he has of squinting with one eye.

But this is the strange part—there's no harness on him, as there is in all the other pictures. Instead, a man is holding what seems to be a rope around Odin's neck, a man wearing a sort of captain's hat. The brim throws a shadow over the top half of his face, so it's hard to see what he really looks like.

"Are you sure that's Odin?" Walter asks, still chewing his wad of cookies.

"I'm positive—" I say, frantic to even imagine why Odin might be with a shady character in Chinatown. But I'm excited too. This is the best *clue* of all in Walter's movie.

I stand up, in my mother's one high heel, and half-limp, half-hop over to Walter Cluster, and practically smother him with a big hug.

And that isn't the weirdest part of a strange day, either. I've just made a total fool of myself, throwing my arms around Walter Cluster, when Miss Pickles says, "Now hush, class. Remember our very special presentation."

And she actually winks at Walter and he winks back. And the whole class is suddenly so quiet, you can almost hear Missy Miles folding her hands together primly on the desktop. It's as if everyone's holding their breath.

"It gives me great pleasure," Walter says, "to announce that *What's Wrong with this Pig-ture?* has been

declared one of the five finalists in the 'Keep Our World Green' contest. I already knew—but I wanted to keep the prize a secret until you all saw the movie. So, we've won a hundred dollars!"

Great big whoops from the class.

I'm trying to sneak back to my seat, but Walter grabs my arm, says, "Hang on, Tammy. Don't go yet. I need you right here beside me."

I blush thirteen shades of pink verging on purple. I can feel the heat in my face.

Walter takes a brown paper bag from behind Miss Pickles' desk, and pulls a brass statue from it—in a beautiful piggy shape. He holds it up then, as if he's just won an Oscar, and rattles it a little. It's a giant piggybank, with a lot of coins inside making a real racket.

More clapping.

Walter explains how he took the check for the prize money to the bank, and asked for a heap of coins when he cashed it.

"For dramatic effect," he says, shaking the piggybank again. "I even put in a lucky penny," he adds, clearly pleased with himself.

Then Walter gives me a strange, secretive look. "I've decided—*we've* decided, everyone who made this movie—that we're giving the prize money to you, Tammy. For running ads, for a reward—whatever you need to find Odin."

The pig doesn't really look like Odin, but the amber glow on the chubby brass cheeks gets me all choked up. I try to turn what feel like soap suds in my throat into hiccups.

"Thanks, you guys," I stammer out. I don't know what else to say.

For the second time in a day I feel good about knowing Walter Cluster even exists. I shuffle toward him, and take the pig in my arms. It's heavy as can be, almost pot-bellied with jangling coins.

Pegga's tippy-toeing beside me in her high heels. I'm traipsing down the sidewalk in my sneakers, big runs in my mother's stockings. Everyone we pass stares after us; the piggybank is making a lovely crashing sound of quarters and nickels and dimes in my backpack.

Pegga's more keen than ever to become an actress now.

"Was I convincing?" she asks. "When I was chasing away those kids who were littering? Or did I just look like myself?"

"You were great," I say. "The whole film was great—because now I can do something to find Odin."

"What?" Pegga asks.

"I don't know yet." But I'm feeling more determined than I have for ages.

I've put the brass pig in the middle of the dinner table, like some sort of wacky centerpiece.

"What's this?" my mom asks, when she finally charges in the door to make supper.

"I can't say until we're all sitting down to eat." But I'm just dying to tell everybody what happened.

I'm so excited, I keep checking the phone messages, to see whether anyone has called about finding a pig. Nothing. I look out the back door too, to see whether Odin has miraculously reappeared in the back yard. It seems like a day for miracles.

My mother's curious to know why I'm so twitchy. It feels as though I've been sitting still for too long, I want to tell her. And now I have a reason to do something. Something important.

Instead I say, "Why won't that stupid spaghetti boil?"

When everyone's finally twirling noodles on their forks, I blurt out what happened at school. The whole thing, with every single detail, including Walter gorging himself on Oreos.

I tell my mom and dad I'm going to Chinatown this weekend, maybe with Pegga and Walter. I try to make it sound casual.

"Maybe I'll do a little Christmas shopping," I say.

"Good plan," Sonja says. "Chinatown's got great bargains—and things you can't get anywhere else."

"I know," I say. Things like Odin, I think.

My dad knows exactly what I'm picturing.

"It's a real long shot, Tammy," he says. "So try not to get your hopes too high, okay? I mean it's been quite some time since Walter took those pictures."

My dad's right. It's been too long already. This can't wait. I'll have to go into the city tomorrow. To Chinatown, to find The Golden Buddha.

13
Bok Choy and Bungee

I'm so nervous that I might miss the early morning train, I go to bed with my clothes on.

11:03: I wake up feeling parched. I trace my fingers in the dark, in an Odin-shape, and then hyperventilate, thinking of my dream with him speaking in Pig Latin, whimpering for help.

1:45: I wake up grabbing and grabbing and grabbing at the shoddy rope around Odin's poor neck—but I can never quite reach it.

3:25: I tiptoe to the kitchen. Like a sleepwalker I find the cookbook with the three twenty-dollar bills that my mom keeps for emergencies. I pocket the whole lot. I have a terrible feeling I might need to buy Odin or pay a reward. That I have to be a millionaire. I fall asleep counting dollars and cents. I'm up over $200, then $300, then I lose track. It seems I will never have enough money . . .

6:35: I have grains of sand stuck behind my eyes. I blink, terrified that I've slept in. I have to hustle to the station with the world's fuzziest case of bed head to make the 7:10 train.

In the bathroom, I notice my dad's jeans, crumpled on the clothes hamper after his shower last night. I shamelessly grab a handful of coins from the pockets. I'll need them for the train fare, I think, forgetting I have a whole stash of change in my piggybank. I'm taking the brass pig with me—for good luck—even though it's hard to lug around.

I slip out the door, walking very, very smoothly to keep the jangling sound in my backpack quiet. Then I really hustle, the weight of the piggybank pressing into my shoulder blades as I jog toward the station. Even running, I can't seem to stop yawning. I make a ching-chang, ching-chang sound as I trot up to the ticket machines. Everyone on the station platform gives me a strange look.

Right then, I almost give up, turn around and go home. What if I *do* find Odin, and he's too weak or skinny . . . what if he doesn't remember me at all? Maybe now he prefers living with someone else. Is happier someplace else.

But it's too late. I'm already on the train, and it's whistling and chuffing into the city. My head's bobbing in that dorky way people fall asleep on buses or park benches. Their mouths start to hang open, and they often start to drool or snore. I almost jump out of my seat when a recorded voice says "Waterfront Station."

It's sunny in Chinatown, almost warm with the bustle of bodies, despite it being late fall. People are poking through the bins at every storefront, shouting out things like "Gooey duck!" and "Tea-smoked chicken!" I see tables of dried ginger root and pickled octopus and Chinese cabbage; it's called bok choy. And tons of yams—it's definitely Odin territory. Small grandmothers fill their string bags with packets of green tea, cans of lichee nuts and water chestnuts, and different kinds of dried mushrooms; some of them pull small shopping carts stuffed to the brim.

The air smells like cloves at Christmas, tangy and sweet at the same time. I walk up Pender Street, under the red and gold archways. Finally I see it, a small storefront with a golden Buddha on the sidewalk, furrowing his brow as though he's doing the world's biggest math question.

There are only a few tables and chairs; it's a teeny restaurant. The front is mostly a bakery, with all sorts of sweets in glass cases. And they even have wedding cakes, like at Howard Wong's, with puff pastry pigs on top.

I point to one of the cakes, and ask a man behind the

cash register, "Have you seen a pot-bellied pig, a live one? Lately, in the last month?"

He smiles at me in a friendly way and nods, as if to say, yes, he agrees that the cakes are nice. "Taste good," he says. He obviously didn't understand my question.

So I take the brass pig out of my knapsack and hold it up—then point outside at the same time. "Have you seen a pot-bellied pig? Outside, on a rope, in front of your store? With a man with a captain's hat?"

I mouth the words slowly, repeat myself like a total dork. The man keeps smiling, even though he's looking confused.

A woman about my mom's age comes over and offers to help. "I'm not sure he knows quite what you're looking for. Do you want me to ask him?"

She's wearing a purple paisley jacket and a lime green skirt. She has a kind face, crinkly orange-blonde hair, and a bad case of bright pink lipstick.

"Do you speak Chinese?" I ask, surprised.

"People here speak different Asian languages: Thai, Korean—not just Mandarin and Cantonese. In this case it's Vietnamese. And I happen to speak a little . . ."

I feel like an idiot.

She introduces herself, says her name's Kristie.

I explain about Walter and the movie, and how the only clue I have of where Odin might be is the picture of him right in front of this restaurant.

Kristie asks the man behind the counter my question

for the third time. It sounds like Vietnamese has a lot of "k" and "q" sounds, up in the roof of your mouth. This time the bakery man understands, but he shakes his head.

"No," he says to me. "No pig. No man with a sailor's hat. I'm sorry." He has a huge line-up of customers, so he turns away.

It's only the beginning of the day and already I seem to have reached a dead end.

"Thanks, anyway," I say to Kristie. But my eyes are brimming up.

I walk down Pender Street, and haven't the faintest idea what to do next. I duck into a small arched door-way with a courtyard beyond. It's quiet and still after the busy sounds of the street, a fountain burbling water gently into a pool holding giant goldfish.

And I start to bawl my eyes out. Great, I think: an almost thirteen-year-old girl, overtired, crying like a baby in the middle of Vancouver. Which only makes me sob harder.

That's when Kristie peeks into the doorway and finds me. "Hi, I'm glad I caught up with you. I could see you were upset."

She sits down with me and doesn't say a thing. Just keeps me company while the fountain bubbles away, and I wipe my eyes, try to pull myself together.

And then I surprise myself. I hear my very own

Tammy voice tell a complete stranger how I took Odin to school and *lost* him on the way home, he was so panicked by the traffic. How *it's all my fault* that Odin is unsafe and miserable, maybe not even—I can't bring myself to say the word *alive.*

Kristie puts her arm around my shoulders and lets me snuffle some more.

"I've never seen your friend Odin," Kristie says. "And I eat at The Golden Buddha sometimes. But maybe we can think of something to do. Let's have some green tea—or maybe you're hungry. Did you have breakfast—do you feel like a snack?"

I shake my head and then nod, a kind of no-yes. My stomach's actually sounding a lot like the fountain. We walk up the street again to the store with the steamy windows and the golden Buddha looking worried.

It's not even close to lunchtime, but Kristie and I indulge, as she calls it. We eat all sorts of little dumplings and spicy green beans and winter melon and pickled cabbage and little cakes made of bean curd until I can't eat another bite.

Kristie tells me she lives in the neighborhood, in Vancouver's smallest house.

"It's like a room with a roof," she says, smiling. "There's not much housecleaning."

I think maybe Kristie's poor to have a house that small, so I shake out coins from my piggybank, to help pay for the meal. We open a couple of fortune cookies.

Kristie reads hers out: "The best prophet of the future is the past."

"What does *that* mean?" I ask.

"I think it means we learn by our mistakes," she says, shrugging. "How about you? What'd you get?"

"Something precious, once lost to you, will soon be returned."

"Wow!" Kristie says, as if I've just won a million dollars. "That's good news, isn't it?"

She's so convincing I almost believe I'll see Odin as we come out onto the sidewalk. But there's just a crush of people, the crowds swelling as if everyone in the city has to rush around, finding their own personal Odin.

Kristie gives me a quick hug, says she has to get to work.

"I work at the food bank, " she says. "And by lunchtime there's always a big line-up. Are you going to be all right now?"

The commuter trains don't start running out of the city again until mid-afternoon. But I don't really want to go home yet, anyway. It feels somehow like I'm abandoning Odin.

Then I have an idea come into my head. It's really Sam's idea, the one about turning bad karma to good. The whole reason he got Odin in the first place. I decide to turn a disappointing day into something better.

"I might as well do some Christmas shopping while I'm here," I say. "I mean, before I catch the train back."

"Good plan," Kristie says. "For some reason, China-town always cheers me up. And I know just the place," she adds, grabbing my arm with enthusiasm. "It's got something for everyone."

She stops at a storefront crammed with everything from colorful kites and paper parasols to whisk brooms and windsocks in the shape of fish. Kristie gives me a card with her phone number at the food bank.

"Come and visit sometime," she says. "Or even help out—we always need people to sort the donations. Every year it seems to get harder to feed everyone, especially around Christmas."

I watch Kristie wave back once at me. Then she disappears into the throngs of people squeezing in and out of the shops.

I think about how kind Kristie was, even though she has all those other people to worry about. At least I'm not feeling hungry—in fact, I'm still stuffed with all the goodies from The Golden Buddha.

And I *do* get cheered up, poking through bamboo floor mats and wicker baskets, feather dusters and beautiful bound notebooks in rice paper. I admire the silk kimonos in rich reds and turquoise, and black-lacquered trays with white and silver flowers, the delicate tea cups and porcelain Chinese spoons.

Kristie's right. You can get almost anything.

On the way back to the train station, I plop myself down on a bench on a small scrap of grass, like some sort of city excuse for a park. I take a look at all the neat stuff I bought. A set of paintbrushes for Sonja, who's been drawing and sketching lately. Green tea and a small red teapot for my mother. It's carefully wrapped in tissue paper inside a wooden box, so it won't get squished by the brass piggybank. For my dad I bought a cookbook of Chinese stir-fry recipes, because he's been puttering around the kitchen lately. And for Pegga I got a small silk shirt, in deep blue, with cloth buttons and a pretty stand-up collar, a gold dragon blazing down the front.

I'm feeling better, as if the whole day wasn't a complete waste. And that's when I see it—parked under a tree, across the park. The truck. White, with a flying red pig—*the* flying red pig—on its side. It makes me feel all goosebumpy just to think it might be the truck that backfired the day Odin ran away. It *has* to be, I think.

I stuff all my goodies into my backpack, and force myself to walk very, very slowly across the measly park. I don't know why it should matter if it *is* the same truck, but it seems important, somehow connected to finding Odin.

The truck is empty, no one near it. There's a parking ticket stuck on the windshield. Up close you can see it's old, a real rust bucket. The white paint is flaking away, and under the flyaway pig is some fancy lettering, so faded I can hardly read it:

PEKING BAKERY : Cakes For All Occasions

I walk around the truck. There are no windows, so I can't see inside. But on the passenger door, a newer kind of lettering says:

UTZ ENTERPRISES
1910 EAGLEVIEW DRIVE
PORT MOODY, BC

Port Moody's just outside the city limits and in the right direction—sort of. It's on the way home, with a slight detour. I run, panting, all the way to the station.

It's only about twenty minutes from downtown to the Port Moody stop because the train's speedy. But it seems to take forever. Then I almost hop onto the wrong bus, I'm so impatient to check out the address.

I have to catch an Eagleview bus that whines and jolts up a steep hillside. We take on and let off a horde of people, little old slowpoke ladies and at least a dozen surly-looking teens who seem to be playing hooky from school too. The bus finally lurches to a stop. The driver points me in the right direction and swears it's only a few blocks.

That's easy for him to say. Every single street seems to curl into another one called Eagleview Crescent or

Eagleview Terrace. I don't know why they name streets like that, all in a bunch. I walk in circles before I finally find the right little loop called Eagleview Drive.

There are only five or six houses, with 1910 smack in the middle at the top of the hill. The grass on the front lawn is tufty and unmowed. The yard's full of junk, things like a bicycle with weeds growing up through the spokes. But what makes this bike special is the chain that tethers it to a rusted metal gate; every single link in the chain is in the shape of a pig. And the rusted metal gate has a cast-iron pig in the middle; and there's a cement birdbath too, full of yucky water. But its base is a stout little pig, as though it's holding the basin on its back. Propped up by the front steps, as though it might have fallen off the roof, is a pig weathervane, the arrow pointing right toward me.

It's the weirdest front yard I've ever seen. Everything shares the same theme. Some wacky collector is mad about pigs.

There's a tarp attached to two posts by the driveway, with one corner hanging down, as though something used to be stored there. I peek underneath, and almost shriek with shock. I see moldy pellets in the dirt, and a rusty old cage the size for a large dog. It's empty, except for some dirty bits of straw. Absolutely empty.

But Odin's been here. I can feel it.

I pull back the edge of the sagging tarp to take a

better look, in case he's wallowed down somewhere out of sight.

"Odie," I whisper, "Hey, Odie, come on here."

And then there's a *zing-zing* sound.

I cup my hand over my right eye—it hurts like *crazy*. A burning feeling, like scalding hot soup. I've been seriously womped by a stretched-out bungee cord hitching up the tarp.

When I lift my hand, my right eye's tearing like mad, as if I'm crying on one side of my face. I see double of everything. Double front doors to the house, where I knock and knock and nobody comes.

I look through the windows on either side of the door, hoping to see Odin's snout pressed up to the thick glass. But all I can see is an umbrella stand with a cane, its handle a carved wooden pig, and a lamp just beyond, with little pigs dancing on their hind legs as part of the design on the shade.

There's a heap of mail dumped on the floor inside, as though no one's been there for days. It's makes me think that whoever lives here, whoever Mr. Utz is, has packed up. Maybe moved away forever. With the pig he kept locked up in that cage.

I press my face against the cool glass of the bus window on the way back down the steep hills. From Port

Moody station, down by the river, I barely catch the 4:30 train out to the valley. I *have* to be home by suppertime or the jig is up, as my mom would say. Meaning, someone can't fake it anymore, they're caught out. Have to fess up.

I'm feeling kind of desperate-but-still-good. It's funny how you can do that, feel two entirely different emotions all mushed together. I'm miserable about not finding Odin; I have a hunch that I was *so close.* But I'm also relieved. That I finally told someone—Kristie— just like that, about losing Odin. That I finally told the truth, even to myself.

The train grinds and grunts its way around corners and into one suburb after another, screeching to a stop, and then swooshing up to full speed again. People are so tired from work, they stare out the windows like zombies, or read paperbacks, each in their own little world. They hardly seem to notice the girl with her right eye half-swollen shut.

For a moment, I let my other eye close too. I can feel the warmth of the afternoon sun slanting through the windows. I fall asleep as the train lurches from side to side, side to side.

Someone trips over me and I startle from my snoozing, say, "Watch where you're going, Odin!"

Everyone gives me a strange look. I stumble off the train just in time. It's sheer luck that I didn't miss my stop.

14
Odin as Oracle

My mom's having nineteen fits when I get home. The first thing she does is put a bag of frozen peas over my eye, and then she starts fuming. It's not exactly shouting, but it's that tone of voice that means she could adopt another kid and maybe replace me.

"You owe us an explanation, Tammy—We were worried sick about you—How could you not have phoned?"

I start to make up some story about helping Pegga move something in her basement and then—whap!—a bungee cord—

My mother cuts me off. "Pegga phoned, wanted to bring over today's homework from school . . ."

And suddenly I'm too tired to lie anymore. I blab out the whole thing—how I couldn't wait for the weekend, had to go into the city to try to find The Golden Buddha.

"And I couldn't find a trace of Odin in Chinatown, or

anyone who'd ever seen him. Or not at first, anyway. But a nice woman who works at the food bank—Kristie —took me for a bite to eat, well, about a hundred bites, and then I—"

I have to stop myself, so as not to give away my Christmas shopping.

"—found the truck, the one with the flying pig," I continue, as if that makes total sense. "And then I took a bus tour—that's what it seemed like, it took ages—to this strange house in Port Moody, with all this junk, like a small piggy theme park . . . And Odin had been there, I was pretty sure—there was a cage and everything. But he wasn't there anymore."

My mother's sighing every two seconds, when she's not repeating everything I say. "Chinatown? Food bank? Flying-pig truck? All the way to Port Moody?"

She can't believe what she's hearing. Neither can Sonja. Her face looks surprised—or maybe it's *impressed*—that her little sister could get into so much trouble.

"You shouldn't have gone to that place alone," my dad says.

"Where, Chinatown?"

"Well, there too. But I was thinking of the strange house in Port Moody."

"I didn't exactly *intend* to go there—it's just that when I saw the truck again, the one that backfired when Odin *got loose* . . ."

I hear myself say it, the beginning of the truth.

I walk over to the cookbook and put the grocery money back. Then I pour a lot of coins into my dad's open hand. "Your pants' pockets," I say.

And then I take a deep breath. I can't stop now.

"You know, Odin wasn't *stolen*. Not at first, anyway. I *lost* him by dragging him to school—it seemed like a good idea for my project. But he got scared on the way home, and I let go of the leash, and he ran off through the traffic. I just want you to know what really happened. That it's *totally, totally* my fault. And that's why I had to fix it. Had to try, anyway."

My mother puts her hand over her mouth and shakes her head. Then she comes over and gives me a big hug—I sniffle into her shoulder. It seems I've run out of tears.

"We knew, Tammy," my mother says somewhere above me.

"What do you mean, you *knew?*" I blurt out, pulling back from the hug.

"Well, we put two and two together. After talking to Miss Pickles, we knew that you'd taken Odin to school. And because you never went back to your classes that afternoon—"

"I knew by the way your story kept changing, as if you'd left part of it out," Sonja says.

I groan.

"How could you guys let me keep on lying?" I ask.

"Especially when I insisted that someone had taken him right from the backyard? I must have looked so pathetic."

Sonja starts to say something again, and then clams up. I'm trying to figure out whether her slight smile is one of pity.

"We knew you couldn't forgive yourself," my mom says. "We could see by your fibbing just how much Odin meant to you. But it was just a simple mistake *anyone* could have made."

I have a brief ridiculous picture of my dad taking Odin to school and lipping off Mr. Bentwhistle, or my mom standing in front of the class in her nurse outfit talking about pot-bellies. I'm trying to picture Sonja running like a lunatic through traffic to save Odin's life, when she suddenly comes over and gives me a nice-sister kiss on the cheek.

"Come on," she says, dragging me to her room. "We'll put on the Odin shade of nail polish, the Brad Pigg color."

I'm still holding cold, soggy peas over my face. But even though I'm dead on my feet and just want to sleep for a week, I don't resist. Sonja paints my chewed-off fingernails a snazzy green with little flecks of gold.

"Just for good luck," Sonja says, admiring her work. She still has a hunch, she tells me, that someday, some-how Odin will be found.

"You *do*?" I ask.

"Yes, I do," Sonja says. She flashes my fingertips around to catch the light.

And for once I don't mind that she sounds so sure of herself.

Once you tell the truth, it's hard to go back. The only kind of lying I've been doing lately is slouching on the living room sofa. Apparently I have some sort of bruise behind my eye, so I have to stay in a darkened room, with no jumping around—not even walking around—and put goopy eye drops in my eye three times a day. Until it heals, which could be weeks.

The doctor gave me a patch for it, so I won't get dust in it, or bang it again. And this way I can watch TV, he said, without straining my good eye. One stays open, and the other just takes a little nap, is how he put it. But it's hard to watch tons of television and keep my head low without getting a kink in my neck. Every day my mom gives me a massage. She says it might be tension, that I need to relax.

Easier said than done. I worry about things I never used to, things like school. I'm so far behind now, it's practically hopeless. I might as well go back to grade seven.

The black patch makes me look tougher than I really am, that's for sure. I feel like a total basket case. Everyone's been extra nice to me, though. Whenever my dad sees me, he tries to lighten the mood. *What have the high seas washed in here—Pirate Tammy?* Stuff like that. And sometimes he pretends to sneak up on my brass piggy in its place of honor on the coffee table, *What ho, is this the pirate's treasure, then?*

"Yeah, sure is," I say, patting the little brass snout glumly.

There's certainly been no one trying to collect any reward. Absolutely nobody's called lately with reports of seeing a maybe-Odin. I guess everyone's too busy making gingerbread houses or hanging Christmas lights to even notice a stray pig. I've tried to keep myself from thinking about it, it's so depressing.

In fact, so far December has been awful. Having to spend days flat on my back, hardly moving, has been so boring I can't believe it. It was almost a relief when Walter Cluster dropped by and did his five-minute version of Shakespeare's play, *Hamlet*. He's doing it for Diana's class. A lot of people get stabbed or poisoned, Ophelia goes mad, and Hamlet can never make up his mind. And Walter plays all the parts. He was making me laugh so hard, I had to ask him to leave.

He walked backward out of the room, bowing and still ranting on like one of Shakespeare's oddball characters, "But m'lady, me thinks thou doth protest too much," and ran smack into my mother.

So my mother invited him in again—just to keep me company, as she said—and he kept talking, nonstop, like a wind-up Walter. About the weirdest things too. Like the experiment they're doing in Mr. Bukowski's science class, about osmosis. It involves potatoes, and some yucky solution.

Walter said, "It's magic, pure magic, the way the weaker liquid moves toward the stronger . . ."

"That's how I feel right now," I said to Walter, pretending to go cross-eyed, my good eye bobbling toward my black patch.

Pegga's always teasing me, as though Walter *likes* me. I tell her Walter's just being himself. He wouldn't know how to flirt even if he wanted to. I can't complain, though; Pegga's been awesome.

She's been taking care of Old Tammy One-eye. Most days all I can do is stare out the window while she goes to school and has fun—I never thought I'd say that. And the weather's been nothing but gray, day after day, with what Pegga calls "fat rain," this kind of sleety slush.

The other afternoon, when it was finally bright and sunny, I pleaded with my mom if I could *please, please, please, pretty-please* go with Pegga over to her house. If I didn't get outside, I'd snap, I told her. Go stark staring mad like Ophelia in *Hamlet*.

"All right," my mom said. "But no hijinks—nothing that might inflame your eye again."

"Right," I said, feeling my way to the front door, taking tiny careful steps, Pegga leading me by the arm.

"What's wrong? Why are you walking like that?" my mom asked.

"Oh, Pegga and I are pretending I'm totally blind," I said. "Just to see what it feels like."

Pegga led me along the sidewalk, saying, "Curb," "Slight hill," "Sharp right turn," as if she were a talking guide dog.

At her house we decided I got my sight back—like some sort of miracle—and we watched a tacky dating show on TV. Afterward we made her three cats into the so-called handsome bachelors. We rated them in looks and gave them personalities, like too cool, or too hairy, or too nervous and jumpy.

She chose her somewhat tubby ginger cat, Mr. Mang, because they shared the same interests, "fine dining, silk cushions, and sunlight." And I chose her skinny, aloof black cat, Salvador, maybe because of Odin liking the one down our street.

"He seems mysterious," I said to Pegga.

"Like Walter Cluster?" Pegga asked.

We hit each other with pillows until feathers were flying all over the place. Pegga's mom had to remind us that I'm supposed to be resting my eye.

"Oops," Pegga said, cleaning up the mess.

Even Sonja's been nice to me, I have to admit. The other day she walks into the garage where Pegga and I were pretending to tell fortunes. Lately I've had this real urge to look into the future. I mean, the recent past hasn't been that great, and the present's still looking iffy, so I need something good to focus on.

"What's the incense?" Sonja asks. "Sandalwood? Nice touch."

We have a kind of crystal-ball-looking lamp, and some of my mom's shawls laid out over the garden chairs. For the right atmosphere. And Pegga and I have made a pot of tea with one of her mom's flaky herbal sort, so that some of the gunk will stick in the bottom of my mother's old English tea cups. Not that we know the slightest thing about reading tea leaves.

"Welcome to the Den of Odin," Pegga says, making her voice sound trancelike, as though she's getting advice from another time and place.

We've propped up Odin's photograph behind the lamp, so that his squinty, know-it-all face seems to loom out of the shadows. And we've made a series of cards, illustrated with flowers and suns and dark clouds zig-zagging with lightning. Most of the sayings are from Howard Wong's fortune cookies, only beefed up a little.

We ask Sonja to pick a card from the half-dozen lying face down.

I say in a quivery voice, "If you chooo—ooose by your right hand, you will not loo-oo-ose."

And then a weird thing happens. Everyone sees it, Pegga and Sonja too. The picture of Odin seems to shiver a little, lift itself up and then settle down again.

As though there's a big breeze in the garage, which there isn't.

"Ooooo, that's spook-k-k-y," Pegga says. Her eyes are so wide she looks like she's seen a ghost through the wisps of incense. Maybe she has. I don't want to think about any *spirit* of Odin, unless he's still around like some sort of pig container for it.

"I think Odin is going to grant your wish," I say quickly to Sonja, wanting to change the subject. I'm suddenly losing my urge to see into the future. I don't even dare look at the Odin-picture again.

Sonja chooses a card and reads out, "Love's vast sea cannot be emptied."

"You know—I think that's right," she says. And she leaves the Den of Odin humming.

"Wow, what's in the tea?" I ask Pegga.

Pegga's mother has dozens of different kinds, made of all sorts of flowers and plants. They're supposed to be remedies for everyday aches and pains and bad moods. Pegga swears they work, too; that some calm you down, and others give you energy on blah days.

"I think this one was Passion Flower," Pegga says. We both look at each other, and say at the same time, "Passion Flower?"

We're giggling away when my mom, who's probably having a cup of her good old, English teabag tea, shouts out to the garage—"Tammy? Mrs. Bing on the phone. About the Christmas bake sale."

Saturday I go down to the mall early. It's nice and quiet on the streets—and it's great to just be walking again, actually swinging my arms and legs, going anywhere. There's a shiny new frost on the ground, and all the trees are sparkling, although there's been no snow yet.

Pet Safe is using an empty store space now that the weather's colder. That way we don't have to pack up our tables all the time. I get there before Mrs. Bing and before all the serious shoppers are out. And shopping's getting frantic, with Christmas coming up fast. So I window-shop a little, making faces at the store dummies looking somehow bored stiff among all the Santa helpers and fake snowflakes.

But there's no more dawdling when Mrs. Bing arrives. I help her pull tray after tray of home baking out of her van, and not just the usual date squares and shortbreads. Some pretty exotic-looking cakes, and gingerbread men too.

"I could have used a larger truck," Mrs. Bing says, and all of a sudden I think of the old Peking Bakery truck, with the flying red pig. I try to block it out.

Next, Mrs. Bing hands me armfuls of newly printed Pet Safe calendars.

"They're not too big—or expensive," she says. "So they'll make good stocking stuffers."

I flip through the pictures of baby llamas up in

mountain pastures in South America and angel fish on a beautiful coral reef in Australia.

"Each animal's in its natural habitat," Mrs. Bing says proudly, as though she put them there herself.

It shocks me a little to see the picture of Odin wearing his hat on the back cover. Even invisible, I guess he's still the Pet Safe Mascot.

"I hope you don't mind," Mrs. Bing says to me softly.

"Not at all," I say. Although it does bother me a bit. It's sad to think that Odin's natural habitat used to be with me.

I have to wince every time a customer who remembers Odin asks about him. They mean well, but it starts to get on my nerves.

"I don't know *how* he is," I have to say, until my lips get numb. "We haven't found him yet."

People tell me stories with happy endings about lost-and-found spaniels and ferrets, even a pair of baby budgies who came back a year later. They'd been living down the street at a neighbor's the whole time.

"Don't give up hope," they say to me, one after another.

I can't tell them that HOPE is the big fat reason I have an Odin shrine at home that freaks out my mother, and hope is the way I got myself womped by a bungee, and hope is why I'm still wearing the eye patch. Not because the sun is too bright or my eye can't see perfectly well again, although it still tears a little sometimes. I wear it just to remind me of almost finding Odin under that tarp, as a kind of good-luck patch. Some people get tattoos of butterflies on their tummies, or pierce their ears a zillion times with different silver studs. In my case, it's a black patch. So what.

It's a bit like that legend about Odin's name. Except in reverse. In this case, *I have to be the brave one,* just for Odin's sake. Brave, and way smarter than I've been in the past.

The bake sale seems to plod along. People stay for a minute and then rush away, as if they just remembered something they have to do before Christmas. I keep eating brownies to make it look as though we might run out, and shake the basket with the fridge magnets of giant pandas. They're too cute to be an endangered species, I tell people. I hand out flyers too, advising against people buying puppies and kittens in the hectic holiday season. I try to look busy, but my heart's not in it. And maybe people can tell.

I slump in my chair and grimace at the strong cup of tea Frank hands me. I put in five sugar cubes, remembering how much Odin liked them.

Then, out of nowhere, Sam walks up. He looks older—maybe it's the haircut.

"I had to get a job after school," he says. "Fast food. So I can save up a little for university next year. And no hairnets were big enough for my mop . . . Besides," he admits, "Sonja likes it better."

I didn't realize they were even talking to each other again. I get a brief picture of them clutching and kissing like they used to, as though they were favorite flavors of ice cream and they couldn't get enough.

"We seem to be getting along," Sam says cheerfully. "We've even gone out again once or twice. Not like a date, but with a bunch of our old friends."

This is news to me—I don't know how I could have missed it. But it explains Sonja being human again. Maybe they've patched it up because of Sonja's fortune of true love—in the Den of Odin. Spook-k-k-ky, as Pegga would say.

Sam gets down on one knee, next to my chair. Puts his arm around my shoulders. He's so close I can smell peppermint on his breath.

"I've still got a good feeling about Odin," he says. "That he'll turn up one day. So don't give up—okay? Promise me." His brown eyes well up as though he could cry right on the spot—whether it's for Odin or for me, I can't tell.

"Thanks, Sam," I say, making a little-kid face, all squished up with feelings of happy and sad.

When Sam walks away I see the strangest thing. I'm probably imagining it, but it looks like the handle of Odin's old leash sticking out of his coat pocket. I must be getting eye strain in the good eye, I think. It might be time to lose the black patch.

15
The Gift of Odin

Christmas Eve.

I know I'm supposed to have all these good feelings for everyone in the whole wide world, but I just can't find them. My mum is humming in the kitchen, the house smells like shortbread, and I wrapped my presents for everyone ages ago—but it doesn't really help.

In fact, I'm feeling the opposite of excited. I'm not even looking forward to eating too much turkey. And I can't imagine opening presents in the morning—not without Odin. All that tissue paper for him to root through. Orange peels galore. For some reason I keep getting this crazy idea he'll be right there with the rest of us, sitting around the Christmas tree. And then I have to snap myself out of it.

I've decided the best parts about glum December were making a Christmas card for Diana, and the day

Pegga and I went into Vancouver to help Kristie at the food bank. We sorted heaps of cans and boxes of Kraft Dinner, that's for sure. We gave out small stuffed animals and books too, for the little kids who came in with their moms and dads to pick up their food hampers. That part was neat, just watching the kids' faces break into big, fat grins.

And Diana actually sent me a Christmas card too, an old-fashioned one with sparkly snow, as if someone had glued sugar on it. She said I could call her over the holidays, and catch up on some of my assignments, if I wanted to.

Strangely enough, I do want to. So I called her up today, and wished her a Merry Christmas. She seemed surprised, *nicely* surprised.

I told her that even though my last assignment will be way overdue by the time school starts again, that I'd still like to learn something about William Shakespeare, and why he's been so famous for so long.

I also thanked her for being so nice about me bringing Odin to school. Most teachers wouldn't have done that, I said, the way she came outside with the class and everything.

"I want to say how sorry I am too, that I caused a fuss with Mr. Bentwhistle, maybe got you in trouble," I added. "I kind of hinted that you'd given me permission to bring Odin . . . I really botched that."

Diana said it took courage to do what I'd done.

"To bring a pig to school?" I asked. I almost blew it right there.

"No, Tammy. To talk to me about that day—and apologize."

I never knew apologies were such a big deal. Months ago I could have apologized for the dirty sofa cushions, the munched nasturtium, the dog-bite trip to the vet's, and maybe everything would have been different.

I'm running all this through my head when the doorbell rings.

I've never seen Sam wearing a jacket. It's a safari type, with tons of pockets, but still. He's looking pretty cool, a red scarf knotted around his neck, his brown eyes as gorgeous as ever.

"I just came by to say happy Christmas," he says.

Sonja looks surprised—she has a towel wrapped around her hair. I wonder whether Sam knows she's streaking it blonde.

"Whatever," Sonja says, trying to stay calm. But she's smiling in a toothpaste ad way, with an on-and-on smile that just won't quit.

"I have something for you," Sam says to her, his eyes crinkling up. And he pulls out a bag from behind his back and gives it to Sonja.

"For Pete's sake, come on in, Sam," my mother says. "You're letting in all the cold air."

"For Sam's sake, come on in," my dad adds, like some corny echo. We all groan.

And suddenly everyone's passing around shortbread and gingersnaps and making all kinds of cheerful small talk. "Taste this—" "How are your parents?" "So, Sam, how's school—got any plans after graduation?"

Sonja takes forever unwrapping her present. It's like she wants to touch the same golden ribbons and red paper that Sam touched for as long as possible.

It's a beautiful sweater. Angora. A sort of deep purply-red with small, gold fishes swimming across her chest. Sonja buttons it up and sighs. It fits her perfectly.

"I didn't know what to get you," Sam says shyly.

There's an awkward silence in the room then. And that's when I hear it. A snorting-and-grunting sound. An Odin sound. I don't want to say anything. Of course I'm just imagining it.

Suddenly everyone in the room is staring at me. And I'm still hearing the soft shnork-shnork-shnork.

"Hang on a minute—" Sam says, as if he almost forgot. "I have something for Tammy too."

He stands up and holds out his hand to me. "Come on, come with me."

I'm turning all red taking Sam's hand, and everyone in the room starts sniggering. I guess the blushing Tammy-girl hearing fantasy pig noises in her head is just too, too funny. It's not funny for me, though. To feel haunted by Odin. I want to run to my bedroom and hide.

Christmas as nightmare. I feel dizzy and sway a little, the room shimmering with colored lights blinking on and off.

"Come on, don't be shy now," Sam says, practically dragging me to the back hall. "I'm sure you'll like this."

At least the ghostly sound of Odin has stopped.

Sam covers my eyes with both his hands and stands close behind me. There's a warm-sweater smell to him, and that minty breath of his right next to my ear. In fact, my whole family is squished into the back hall. We couldn't be much closer unless the five of us were squeezed into a phone booth.

"Open the door—" Sam says to someone, and I hear the door to the garage squeak the way it always does. Then Sam lifts his hands away from my eyes.

I blink and gasp. He's a little thinner, looks smaller somehow. But he has that tilt to his head, the gleam in one eye, and that squint in the other. It's Odin.

He's all dressed up in gold garlands, a small sprig of mistletoe in his hat. He's wearing a smart new Hudson's Bay blanket. Custom made by the look of it—it fits perfectly. Cream wool with the bright yellow, red, green and indigo stripes. Dapper is Odin. Wonderful is Odin.

I drop to my knees in front of him and he grunts, then curls up his nose as though he disapproves of all the fuss.

"How'd you find him? Where—?"

"It's a long story," Sam says. "Let's just say a certain Mr. Utz finally phoned Mrs. Bing, and Mrs. Bing asked me to check things out. First of all, you have to picture Mr. Utz; he's this gnarly little man who blinks his eyes all the time. Acts kind of jumpy and nervous. He said Odin had trotted up the rickety old ramp into his truck that day—he had the back door open unloading something. And he couldn't see anyone *with* the pig, so he'd just taken him home.

"Mr. Utz swore he never saw our ads in the paper, or not at first. Besides, he said, he'd really grown to like Odin, wanted to keep him, because he was well-trained, would do almost anything for grapes—

"I don't think the feeling was mutual, though. Once I saw the condition Odin was in, too miserable to eat much, with almost no tummy at all, if you can imagine—"

I don't want to imagine a skinny Odin.

"He'd been feeding him mainly birdseed and canned dog food and stale bread crusts—not exactly the right diet for a pot-belly. But I guess he didn't know better, or didn't have a lot of money. And I'm sure Odin was lonely too—I think he missed you, Tammy."

"You didn't pay him a reward, did you?" I ask indignantly.

"Well, I guess Mr. Utz finally admitted to himself that it didn't seem fair to keep Charlie—that's what he called Odin. He was away at work a lot, leaving Odin by himself in that cage, and that's why he called Pet Safe. So I figured he deserved something—at least he was honest and tried to do the right thing, even if it was a little late. But I didn't even know what the reward was—"

We all look at each other. Beyond the hundred dollars in the piggybank, donated by Walter, we hadn't ever thought about it. What we might have given to get Odin back. Two hundred dollars? Five hundred dollars? Nine hundred and ninety-nine dollars?

"So I just cleaned out my wallet—gave him forty-five bucks. He looked a little grumpy about that—at least until he saw how Odin waddled over to me like a long-lost friend, grunting and humming, the way he does when he's overjoyed. He was pressing up against my legs, practically purring . . . So that was that.

"I'd just gotten him back before your wild goose chase to Port Moody. And I wanted to make sure he was healthy first before you saw him. And that took awhile, and then it was almost Christmas, so . . ."

As if he doesn't want to hear any more of the story, Odin pushes past me into the house, his legs swishing with prickly garlands.

"Well, look who's making himself right at home," my mother says, and everyone laughs. And that laugh, everyone so happy, suddenly changes a dull, dismal December into my favorite one ever.

I grab a couple of mincemeat tarts for Odin and stick

a candy cane into my cheek. Soon Odin's making a mess, dropping pastry out of both sides of his mouth.

Sam does an Odin face, pushing up his nose and making his eyes into slits. Odin does it right back at Sam, as though they've been practicing. For a minute it's a toss-up. Cute rules, and I don't know who to choose: Sam or Odin.

Just for a joke, Sam hands Odin's leash to Sonja. Like he did last summer. But now Sonja takes the leash with a flashing smile. It's like she's passed some sort of love test, with my mom and dad and me and Odin as witnesses.

"Very funny," I say, and hustle Odin out of the room, before anyone gets any bright ideas about Odin being a big, fat friendship ring.

When Sam leaves, Odin and I are already hunkered down in my bedroom, one of my blankets twisted up in a comfy knot beneath his big fat football shape. He's snoring softly.

My mother opens the door a crack.

"If you think Odin is staying inside, you're wrong," she whispers. "It will only give him the wrong impression."

"I won't let him up on the bed," I promise. "And at least he doesn't shed. Think of it—Sam could have brought a guinea pig, or a Himalayan cat—but I'm glad he didn't," I add.

"That's not what I meant," my mother says, coming a little farther into the room. "We have to have a family pow-wow tomorrow. Keeping Odin will mean everyone in this house will have to pitch in . . . especially as he got into some bad habits when he was away."

"Like what?"

"Well, let's just say he's not as housebroken as he once was. And he chews things now—rugs, shoes. Or so Sam warned us. So we'll have to come up with a sensible plan, especially in winter."

I'm sitting bolt upright now, cold, clammy alarm flooding my body.

"I'll train him, I'll fix him . . ." I say fiercely. "Please don't tell me that he can't stay here—with me—no matter *what* he does. Please, Mom. Don't."

"We're going to do our best, all of us, to make sure he's happy. But you're deluding yourself if you think you can keep barely scraping by at school, with Odin being your main concern—"

I see my mother's mouth moving: she's saying something about New Year's and making promises to do better. But I don't hear the actual words. I have a terrible sinking feeling. That we're right back where we started: that Odin's nothing but a problem, and I have to prove he belongs with me, in this family, right where he is.

"Please take Odin to the garage now, Tammy," my mother whispers. "I didn't mean to upset you," she adds. "Everything will work out, you'll see."

She gives me a quick kiss on the forehead. "Sleep tight, sweet dreams," she says, and turns down the hallway.

Merry Christmas to you, one and all, I say under my breath.

I grimly put on my hoodie and fleece vest over my flannel jammies, and pull my sneakers over my bare feet. I stuff a wool hat on my head, and drag the sleepy Odin to his feet. He's reluctant to leave my littered room. It's practically paradise for him, rolling around in my cast-off clothes on the floor. Especially after all the horrible things that must have happened to him, like living in that nasty cage.

I catch a glimpse of myself in my dresser mirror. I slip on my black eye patch again—it makes me feel stronger somehow.

I can't bring myself to just stick Odin into the garage and abandon him. Not on Christmas Eve. No sir, we're going to spend some quality time together.

Odin moans his way to the back door with me, his hard little feet slip-sliding down the stairs. His stomach isn't sagging enough to make that steel-wool scraping noise over the treads. I make a note to myself to fatten him up a little. Or even a lot.

There's a wind kicking around the leaves in the

backyard. The stars are bright over our heads, and some group of keeners is singing Christmas carols up and down the block. Odin and I can hear them going from house to house. Odin sings along softly, off-key as usual.

"I am not *deluded*," I say to Odin. But despite wanting to stay mad at my mother, I find myself humming along to "Good King Wenceslas" too.

We slip into the little roofed cubbyhole that holds the garbage cans, behind the garage. Odin flops himself down with a begrudging grunt across my feet, as if to keep them warm. Odin as Furnace. Another good reason to keep Odin, I think. I start to run a list through my head.

First off, the number one, big-time reason.

1. *He makes me happy.*
2. *He makes other people laugh too, which is the best ever sound in December.*
3. *He's the Pet Safe mascot. They need him to do their good work for other animals just like Odin. So there. That one should be totally obvious.*
4. *Because of Odin, I'm a volunteer—at the food bank in Vancouver now too, with Kristie, as well as at Pet Safe.*
5. *He's a useful composter, and always will be. So he's good for the environment—and good for projects about the environment.*
6. *He's the reason I got an A in English for once. So there's a chance he can make a better student out of me yet.*

7. *He's a natural film star, as in Walter Cluster's movie.*
8. *He makes me tell the truth—eventually. It's because I take him seriously as my responsibility. And I actually want to take care of him. And that's led to me taking better care of other things too, like cleaning up my room, trying to make supper—okay, I'm not so good at cooking or tidying, but still.*
9. *He changes bad karma to good, just like Sam said. In fact, Sam and Sonja might be all lovey-dovey again just because of Odin's strange power to make things come out right.*
10. *And the last and probably best reason I can think of to keep Odin—even though I sometimes forget about him being stubborn or sensitive—is because **I make HIM happy**.*

I start to repeat the whole list again, so I can rhyme it off to my mother tomorrow, when we have our family meeting on the topic of Odin. The cold slips inside my jacket and starts to hum in my ears.

At midnight—or so it says on my watch—my teeth are actually chattering. Odin and I must have dozed off.

I can hear my mother calling out into the yard—"Tammy? Tammy? Can you hear me?" Where are you?" She's trying not to shout too loudly and wake the neighbors, I guess. But her whispery kind of shouting makes her sound helpless, almost frightened.

I'm fine, though, and should really let her know that. But for some reason I'm feeling a little light-headed, almost giddy. And can't just jump to my feet. In fact, my feet feel a little numb, or squashed, underneath Odin. I wiggle them a little.

Odin whimpers, then lets out a small yip-yip, as though he wants to be found.

"Shhhhh . . . What was that?" I hear my mother say to someone. There's talking, someone that sounds like my father, a door slamming.

"You and your big snout," I whisper. I press my hands down over Odin's muzzle and he looks peevishly up at me. He narrows his eyes, as if to say, *I'm not sorry. Not in the least.*

I can hear footsteps approaching through the frozen leaves. Crunch. Crunch. Crunch.

"Tammy, what were you thinking?" my mother asks.

"I was thinking you might not let me keep Odin after all," I say sheepishly. "And then I reviewed all the good reasons I could think of—to convince you. And the list of reasons to keep Odin was quite long. So long, I guess I fell asleep."

"Oh, Tammy, you react so fast sometimes. I never said you couldn't keep Odin. That's not what I meant at all."

I can see both our faces in the bathroom mirror. My black eye patch looks ridiculous, I have to admit.

"Why are you wearing that again?" my mother asks, gently taking it off.

"It has something to do with an old legend, with a god-Odin in it. He loses the sight in one eye in order to be true to what he believes. His name means *Wish.*"

"Oh, I didn't know that," she says.

She keeps dunking my right hand into a sink of luke-warm water. Just in case I have a touch of frostbite.

"I'm fine," I keep repeating.

"Why didn't you put your hand into your pocket?" she asks.

"I was nervous about letting go of Odin's leash," I say, and start to sniffle.

My mother's eyes are puffy, and her throat has a catch in it, like she might be getting a cold.

"Your father was about to go out looking for you," she says to the girl in the mirror. "When he couldn't find you in the garage, he was trying to figure out where you'd gone. He thought that with Odin tagging along, you couldn't have gone far."

"So Odin's a good thing," I murmur. I smile slightly. The girl in the mirror smiles back.

Odin is lying on the bathmat—he likes the steamy air of the hot water running. He is flipping his tail around in relief at having been found. This time, so close to home.

EPILOGUE
Ten Good Reasons

There's an epilogue to every story. That's what Walter says. A way of looking back at what was happening when you were right smack in the middle of things.

Walter figures Mr. Utz might be an intriguing character, with a lot of different sides to him. "In a Shakespeare play, people are tragic because of who they *might have been,*" he says.

Of course it's difficult to know just exactly who Mr. Utz might have been, I mean before his yard was all overgrown and his old bakery truck started to backfire.

"I think it might be interesting to know why he started collecting all that pig paraphernalia," Walter adds, like he's some sort of psychologist now.

"What's paraphernalia?" Pegga asks.

"It's just a big word for junk and stuff," Walter explains.

"So why didn't you just say junk?" Pegga and I chime at Walter.

But I don't think all of the weird things at the Port Moody house were useless junk. Neither does my mother. We are now the proud owners of the birdbath, with the cement piggy holding it up. It sits in our back yard, all cleaned up, and birds are always swooping down to flap around in it.

Mr. Utz gave us the birdbath. Phoned us up and said we could take whatever we wanted from his yard, that he was putting the place up for sale and needed to tidy up.

My dad went with me to poke through all the stuff. That's when he made an offer on the piggy-truck. He thinks he got a real steal for a couple of hundred dollars.

"It's a win-win situation," my dad said. "I get a real beaut . . . well, once I fix it up a little—and Mr. Utz gets a new lease on life. Or we hope so."

Mr. Utz had used the truck to do odd jobs for people: moving clunky furniture from their attics, or carting away bags of leaves in the fall. He was scrambling to make any kind of money, even though he was old enough to be retired. And now he's moving to Florida to live with his sister.

I never actually met Mr. Utz in person. My dad dropped a check for him through the mail slot, and the next day Mr. Utz left an envelope on the right front wheel, under the fender. With a key in it. And surprise,

surprise, the old truck started and churned its way into traffic.

I wasn't too sure whether Odin would be glad to see it parked at our house. But I've already taught him how to get in and out of the back door; my dad built Odin a nifty new ramp with slats, so his feet won't slip. I figure it's another case of turning bad karma to good. Grapes up the ramp, and grapes on the down slope.

That was another surprise: Mr. Utz left a small donation inside the truck. The envelope said, "For Charlie: The Pig Who Liked Grapes." There was one tattered twenty-dollar bill inside, and a bunch of store coupons for things that Odin mostly doesn't eat, like sweet cereals and TV dinners. But I guess Mr. Utz was feeling guilty about Odin being cooped up in a cage, and not feeding him properly.

It's funny how things turn out. People actually being better than you first think.

Like Walter Cluster, for example. I've gotten used to Walter and his strange outbursts. That way he has of always knowing something I think I don't care about—at least until he makes it seem somehow interesting.

"Maybe you'll end up being a teacher," I said to him the other day. Most kids his age would take that as a total insult. "I mean a good one, like Miss Pickles," I added quickly.

"I'm tickled pink," he said, making his voice all

fluttery and cheerful, just like Diana's. Well, it gave Pegga and me giggle fits.

The three of us were scraping the Mr. Utz letters off the truck, and painting on new ones with a stencil kit Pegga had brought over. Turns out Walter still wants to make that Halloween horror movie. He has it in his head he's going to have Odin glowering out the window of the pigmobile—as if he's driving. Like some sort of madman—or in this case, mad pig.

I can just picture Odin squinting through the windshield, tooting his *wanhoo—wanhoo* horn and squealing out his version of "Road hog!" to anyone who gets in the way.

Now the passenger door on our maybe-movie truck reads:

ODIN ENTERPRISES
1411 PLUMTREE PLACE

That's as far as we got before we ran out of Sonja's greeny-gold Brad Pigg nail polish. My dad doesn't mind that we were goofing around; he has to totally repaint the old clunker anyway.

"Ee-say ou-yay ater-lay!" Walter shouted back at us, as he was leaving.

"See you later, too, Alter-Way!" we hollered after him.

"Do my ears deceive me, or were you kids talking in Pig Latin?" my dad asked, as Pegga and I clattered into the house.

I slapped him on the back, and said, "That's right, Pop-sicle!"

I might have to stop saying that soon; it seems too little-kiddish since I turned thirteen.

I got really great presents, even though it was only three days after Christmas, when everyone's groggy with too much yummy food and never wants to go shopping again. Everyone except Pegga, that is. She forced me to go with her and try on some new clothes. So I spent some of my birthday money on comfy cords—and a wide belt to go with them. With small, silver bells on it, so I jingle when I walk.

And Sonja gave me some rusty-purple nail polish that she swears is all the rage—she said it would keep me from biting my nails. Sam gave me a tetherball for the backyard—it's actually for Odin, so he can bunt the ball on the rope around with his snout and keep trim. It's definitely a spectator sport; we laugh our heads off at Odin's best moves.

Christmas—and turning thirteen—already seem lifetimes ago. Sonja says time seems long and all stretched out at the beginning of something—and then it snaps back, seeming only an instant, when you think back afterward.

"Like a bungee going *zap-zap?*" I ask, with this shame-on-me look on my face.

"That's right," she says, giving me a not-too-hard sister-pinch.

Maybe one day I'll look back to grade eight and just think of Diana being a neat teacher and my mother being shocked that I went *all the way to Port Moody!* and Walter Cluster making one of his weird comments and Pegga and me wearing high heels to the film *pree-miere*, and the rest will vanish.

Which is an odd thought. Especially when I think how torn apart I was about losing Odin.

He's wearing his new fedora at a too-cool slant on his fat forehead these days. That was the best part about Christmas for me, I think. That there was a present for Odin under the tree.

I guess Mom didn't even need my *Ten Good Reasons*.

We've made a deal: she'll keep her promise about letting Odin live with us forever, until he's a grumpy old pig, if I keep mine about getting better marks at school. How hard can it be, I figure, if I get more organized, and don't leave things for the last minute. And somehow get a new brain for math.

Last week, Odin and I went down to the mall for the spring Pet Safe parade. I got to be one of the judges for "Smallest Pet, Fuzziest Pet"—fun stuff like that, just so little kids get to bring along their hamsters and kittens and learn all sorts of nifty things about animals. One boy even brought along a spider in a teeny aquarium, and knew heaps about "arachnids," as he called them. He'll probably be another Einstein or something.

I felt good about giving Mrs. Bing the prize money

from Walter's film. Everyone who made the movie agreed that was fair, because it was the mascot picture of Odin in the paper that helped him get home.

I wonder sometimes how time seems to pass for Odin. I think he has a calendar in his head—or maybe it's more of a scrapbook—made of plums or good naps, or happy times round the family table. He's allowed inside now when we eat, like a real member of the family. And he lies there, on the oval rug, grateful as can be.

Of course Odin's had a few tricks up his sleeve all along. Last night my mom admitted, in front of everyone, that she'd actually been letting Odin into the kitchen way back when. She'd leave the door unlatched so that he could pretend to push his way into the house. And she'd have these "little chats" with him too.

I have to say, the idea of my mom talking to Odin, well, it totally surprised me.

"Watch this," my mom said. "I've found a great new scratching spot on his belly."

And sure enough, if Odin didn't do a demonstration, right on the spot. He lifted up a back leg as though he might topple forward onto his nose. That was the cue for my mom to get down on the floor and give Odin a tickle. I couldn't believe my eyes.

I guess we all have our secrets. And if we're lucky, we get to share them.

Acknowledgments

Every book is a journey and I'd like to thank my guides along the way. First, Annick Press for their unswerving commitment to this project from the sizzling idea stage to completion; Barbara Pulling, Pam Robertson, and Elizabeth McLean for their valuable help in process; Sonja Mulabdic for the inspired illustrations; Jung Wha Lee for gracious tidbits in lunch and language. Kudos to my generous clan of good friends for shoring me up with food and fellowship whenever I was frazzled.

My deep thanks, as ever, to Ann and Lyman Henderson for the precious gifts of time and good faith required to write a story. And my gratitude to Tim and Gail Dundas for sharing their many fine moments of family by way of plums with Odin. Thanks, Alexis, for all your funny and insightful versions of "staying grounded," including Tipping Mother Tree Pose.